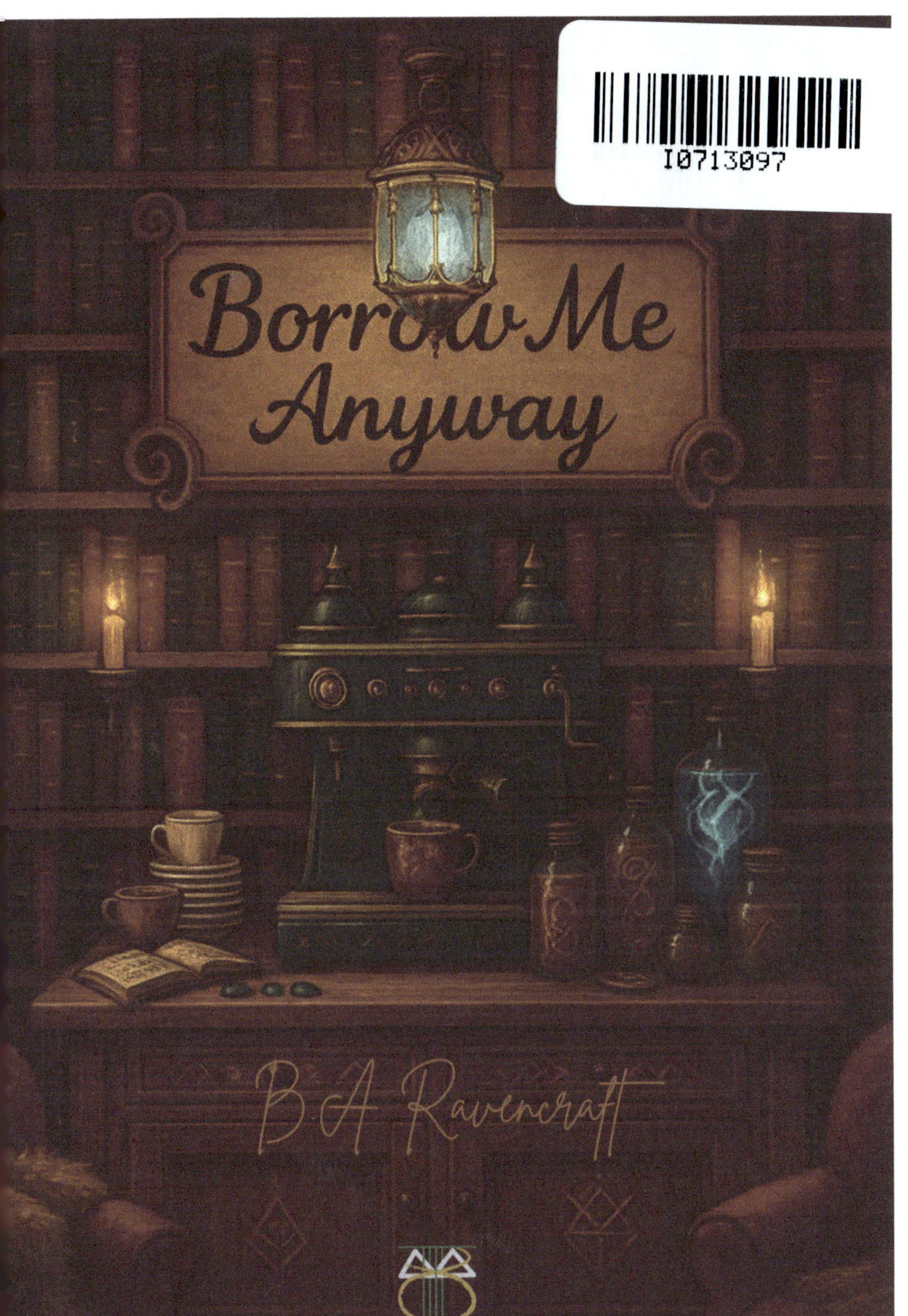

Borrow Me Anyway
B A Ravencraft

Please

Note

This is my kind of a cosy-fantasy, so they're all a little traumatised but it's how they come together that create that warm cosy feeling we all know and love. Please read the short list below and be sure this is for you...

- Trauma - more than you expect

- Narcissists

- Mental Health Discussions

- Healing Journeys

The characters and scenarios described within are entirely fiction and the opinions expressed therein, while thought provoking do not in anyway represent the thoughts or feelings of the Indigenous Aboriginal Peoples of Australia at large.

For Aboriginal and Torres Strait Islanders, while this book does feature inspiration from a variety of traditional stories, they do not in any way infringe upon the Sacred Histories of any Aboriginal Tribe. Australia is unceded Aboriginal Land and this book is a complete reflection of this.

Always Was, Always Will Be

One

A nother day, for another dollar. That was what her grandmother had said every morning that she'd woken up in their guest room.

"Come on darling, it's time to get up, it's another day for another dollar."

Being the eternal disappointment of her family was the most sentimental she'd ever managed to be when she thought about home. Hayden was just like any other girl, wanting to leave her mark on the world. She just didn't want that mark to mar the beauty of what already existed—falling in love with everything new she learned. Knowledge was her most favourite thing that consciousness had managed to birth, well, that and coffee.

Years of studying and working in university libraries had only deepened that love further still—both for caffeine and knowledge. She'd managed to finally get her thesis published in none other than *Archives and Museum Informatics* just last year, earning herself a PhD in Archiving.

Unfortunately none of the museums, or archiving institutions were hiring particularly often since she wasn't a research student any more. That had put her out of the university dorms and straight into her grandparents' guest room. For the six months she'd managed to last, all Hayden heard was how well her older brother—the public relations and marketing king—was doing at work, and being reminded that she was only able to stay until her grandparents went on their cruise. So she needed to find a rental or move back in with her mother.

Instead, Hayden responded to that final ultimatum by purchasing the shack she now called a home, on the dry and half-barren land she now called her homestead. A move that took both most of her savings as well as having brought her half a world away from the hectic city she'd grown up in.

While most people would be petrified at moving so far away from everything they'd ever known, to Hayden, this was simply her next big adventure.

Now, as she sat in the plasterboard enclosed living room she thought about the sheer expense the drywall had cost. Hayden had thought that the bulk of the cost would have come from hiring help, little had she realised that plasterboard was just as pricey. The small fortune in building supplies had drawn into stark realisation that if she didn't get a paying job soon, she may just wind up crawling back to her mothers' house after all.

The quiet country town of Abernathy, New South Wales, was tiny by comparison to the sprawling metropolis she'd grown up in. Unfortunately, the cost of living crisis that had forced Hayden into buying the run-down plasterboard home, had affected the country town even more so. Of the seven positions the local employment office had managed to find, she had already applied for three of them, with interviews already pending for the other four.

Hayden didn't hold much hope for them though, all of them wanted someone with experience in agriculture. There wasn't much use for her PhD in the hardware store or on farms.

The feeling of dread began to sink in as she recalled the last time she'd seen her mother. It was as she waded through the piles of boxes precariously stacked in her parents' garage, attempting to find the last few boxes of her childhood belongings.

A box of memorabilia in her arms and exhaustion etched in every line of her mothers eternally disappointed face as she watched Hayden continue to dive through the stacks of family history.

"I just don't understand why you don't just stay here and get a job doing what you love, isn't that why you spent almost a decade at uni? Don't you want a chance to use your degree so you can pay back your student debt?" Lileth pleaded once more, "Come on love, surely you don't want to spend all your hard earned money on this half-baked idea only to not be able to get a paying job and end up having to move back into your old room anyway."

"Mum, stop—I've already spent the money, I paid the whole thing straight away. Besides, I'd rather just buy my own derelict place on an amazing amount of land, than spend the same money on a granny flat here, just because I might be able to get a job. Besides, I thought you said I wouldn't have to worry about paying back my tuition fees because as long as I was studying I was your dependent?" Hayden replied bitterly.

"I wasn't talking about your fees Hayden, I was talking about the money you borrowed from your brother to help pay for the cost of all those holidays you took during your studies. He deserves to be reimbursed for that." Lileth dismissed.

"What holidays—wait, do you mean when I went to Greece for my archeology units? What money?"

Confused about what her asshole older brother had somehow convinced their mother of doing, she'd snatched the box from her mother and stormed out of the house leaving the rest of her things behind.

She'd found the rest out from her grandmother later that evening. Apparently, while she had picked up jobs working at the various cafes, bookstores and newsagents on the university campus had meant absolutely nothing to her parents—who had been entirely convinced that it had been Paul who had paid for all the travel and expenses that her studies had forced her to take.

Between the scholarships Hayden had managed to land to cover her own cost of living while studying, she'd chosen to live in a dorm on campus and use her meal card for her own cost so that she was able to take on extra jobs around the university. Saving every cent had meant that her entire economy-style travel and staying in a hostel while working on her international studies was debt-free.

So furious that in the decade of conversations, no one had ever even thought to verify that what Paul had said was true, Hayden had called a removalist to pick up the past of her things while she loaded her most precious necessities into her beat-up Subaru. She'd left that night, her grandmother didn't believe her so why stay?

It had taken almost the entire day to reach Abernathy, but at least she'd managed to end the day in her own home.

The morning following the final installation of the plasterboard in her living room, Hayden readied herself for the job interview at the hardware store in town. Hoping that the small bit of retail she'd done while working at the university's textbook store would be enough to secure the position. Knowing that the only reason any of the farmers would hire her was out of pity, she preferred the simplicity of a limited experienced position, over the no experience chaos of becoming a farmhand.

The irony that the whim on which had brought her to town being the fantastical ideal of building her own farmstead and house out in the wilds of Australia, while having absolutely no practical skills was not lost on her. Especially as she talked herself through the potential questions the store manager may ask her about the lack of relevant experience and knowledge regarding farming and building supplies.

It was almost ten in the morning as she pulled into the locally-owned hardware store. A rare thing in the current economy, Hayden thought to herself.

A warm sensation crossed her chest as another unique little quirk of this country town made her fall just a little more in love with it. All her life she'd had this ridiculous little fantasy of living in one of those Hallmark towns--completely ridiculous, but the absolute nostalgia of a "mom & pop" hardware store in a little country town chipped away just a little chink in the staunchly cynical heart Hayden had been forced to adopt while growing up in the city.

Walking up to the sales counter, Hayden adopted her best smile while attempting to appear relaxed and confident.

"Good morning," She greeted warmly. "Morning, can I help you find anything today? Ready for some spackling plaster to finish off that room you're working on?" The clerk at the counter asked.

"Wow, you remember me from the other day?" Hayden asked excitedly.

"Of course, I delivered your drywall sheets, remember? It's okay, my name's Jayne--my dad owns the store. How's the room coming, anyway?" he replied, instantly making her feel comfortable.

"Great actually, I finished putting it up yesterday, but I'm actually here for an interview with your Dad this morning for that position that's available?"

"Brilliant! Dad'll be happy about that, just so you know it's only a bit of part-time work. There's a large chain-store that opened up a couple of years ago about an hour away. At first nobody went 'cos it was so far, but since the market crash we just haven't been able to compete with their prices." Jayne said sheepishly.

"Honestly, with the amount of work I think my house is going to take, I don't think I'm going to have more than that much time to offer. As for the pay, I really don't need a lot to survive on since I don't have a mortgage—I'll just DIY the rest so I can save on costs for the fixes." Hayden laughed happily.

"Really? Cool, Dad's in his office at the back of the store. I'll show you, and then we can see about finding you some spackle so you can finish off that living room of yours."

Jayne led her down the isles of power tools and various hardware to what appeared to be a fairly open staff kitchen and living area with a large window into the store managers' office. Jayne pointed her to the coffee pod machine and the living chairs, then left to return to the store's front counter.

Feeling like the coffee is a test, Hayden instead chose to help herself to a tall glass of water, taking a seat opposite the window. She took a casual sip and put her glass to the side, choosing to look through one of the many hardware magazines on the coffee table. Casually reading through a couple of the articles to gain a bit more insight into the hardware-world, she quickly found herself immersed in looking through the decor and design section when she heard her name being called.

"Hayden? Mind if I join you?," the older man, Charlie, she remembered, asked. "Good morning, drive in alright? Excellent." He continued as she nodded her reply while he took the seat opposite her.

"I know Jayne's already spoken to you, he threatened to do just that earlier this morning when I told him I was going to hire some more help." Charlie began, "the truth is I can only really afford to pay anyone about six-hundred-dollars a week. It's not much more than a couple of days work a week, but you'll get to choose the majority of your hours. I just really need a hand on Sunday mornings for a few hours while Jayne is at football and on Wednesday afternoons while he's at practice. After that you can work out the rest of your hours with Jayne so that you can give him a bit of down time. The last thing I want is for his whole life to become about this place, when I can't even afford to give him a weekend off."

"I'll be honest, I don't really need much, but there's plenty of time left in the day to get another part-time job. I can promise that I won't go behind your back to the chain-store an hour away —and not just because I have no idea how to get there." Hayden joked.

"I read over your resume, you're more than overqualified so you can have the job —it's not hard, just re-stocking shelves and helping the stray customers find what they need. For paint mixing and building supplies we have trade hours that we do those in, so you won't need any specialist training. Have you thought about heading over to Borrow Me though, and seeing if they could use someone?" he suggested as he finished explaining the position.

"There's a bookstore in town? I had no idea, when I googled this place after finding the ad for my house I couldn't find anything about one." Hayden babbled.

"Well, not exactly, it is a bookstore but they encourage borrowing more than buying. You should speak to Jason when you get there, he's in charge of the cafe'" Charlie suggested.

Once confirming her start shift for after the holiday period had ended, Hayden headed off to collect her spackle and attack the holes in her living room feeling truly accomplished for the first time since receiving a copy of her journal article months ago.

Two

A couple of days' later she had heard back from the farmhand positions she had applied for; none had felt she was the right person. They were right of course, but that still left her quite a bit short of being able to finish fixing-up the fibro-house to a state that she could actually live in.

When the intake pipe from the rainwater tanks burst that morning—and the last hope of a hot shower to wash off the sweat from Haydens' pathetic attempt to fix it disappeared—she headed into town to see if the local bookstore had a copy of *Plumbing for Dummies*.

Borrow Me bookstore and cafe was the coziest looking bookstore Hayden had ever seen. It had been the hardest place in town to resist entering—despite the fact that she had been in town for a little over a month now—her ever tightening budget and increasing list of bills had meant that the risk of purchasing unnecessary literature was an absolute no.

Today, however, meant emergency services were necessary since she still didn't have a satellite yet and her phone's service was spotty on the best of days. So, as she walked through the ornately carved wood and glass front doors for the first time, she was hard-pressed not to simply stop and stare at the sight before her.

Wall to ceiling, double story bookshelves encased the room on either side. The only interruption being the huge lead-lined windows, bathing the entire central space with natural light. An iron-railed staircase led to the upper balcony where it was easy to see the stacks of book cases, reading nooks, desks and shared reading areas dotted across the space above. A cafe counter and access to the kitchens beyond with what appeared to be a re-purposed vintage credenza being used as a counter and barista station servicing the space opposite the double-doored entrance Hayden had stepped into.

Continuing into the front space, she headed to the **Borrowing** counter to the left of the entryway, where a short brunette with thick curls sat, seemingly talking to someone on her earbud.

As she drew closer she noticed the tell-tale signs of her *Eternal Nature*, the subtle lines of swirls and bark echoing within her lightly-tanned skin. The realisation that she was about to talk to an actual tree-spirit dawned on her. Working in the university library had limited her interactions with people in general, but everyone knew how little the *Immortals* enjoyed living in the cities—she had simply never had the opportunity to meet someone *Immortal* before.

The excitement caused her to falter slightly over the small step up to the service counter, making the clerk look back from the shelves.

"Hello, you're new," she said bluntly.

"Hi, yeah, I just got to town a few weeks ago. I'm living in that old fibro-house out on Old Blacktop Road." Hayden explained pleasantly.

"Well duh, no one else would take so damned long to come in here. What do you want?" from the tone she was using, it seemed that Haydens' reticence to come into the store had been noted. Not the impression she had ever wanted to set with the local bookstore, let alone one of this wonder.

The light shining in through the windows shifted from the golden haze she'd driven through, to a blue-tinged echo—rain was on the way. But the feel within the store shifted, from the inviting warmth and wonder as she'd entered, to an almost cold sadness.

Feeling the innate need to defend and explain herself she turned back to the clerk. "I'm so sorry, between trying to find a job and my house falling apart I haven't had a lot of time. Well, that and I knew I'd walk out of here broke. I love books but I just don't have the money at the moment to really splurge."

The light in the clerks' eyes sent warmth through to her soul; searching and honest, finding the same echoed in Haydens' eyes the clerk smiled and just like that the mood in the store shifted once more.

"Okay, you're forgiven, but only if you don't stay away this time. You don't have to buy a book to come in here, that's the whole point of Borrow Me. Here, we have an extensive range of books you can borrow." She began to explain, "Every time a customer orders a new book, we buy an extra—no matter how much it destroys my soul to do so. This way we have an ever increasing amount of books that no one has to buy, but can read while enjoying any number of things. Including the incredible food, made by our in-house *Immortal* chef, Patrick."

"Wow, that's incredible, I promise, I'll never stay away again! What's your name, you never said?" queried Hayden.

"Oh my Gods! You can't just ask an *Eternal* what their name is! Don't you know anything about namelore?" She screeched suddenly, then burst into laughter. "Just kidding, I'm Siobhan, that big guy over there singing is Jason, don't be scared he's a sweetheart, and over there at the sales counter is Daniel."

"Huh, I've never met a Minotaur before, he's got an incredible voice. How's the coffee?" She wondered aloud.

"Oh, it's the best in the southern hemisphere honestly. The only thing is the machine doesn't work unless Jason is in fact singing, so if he's got a sore throat and can't perform then everyone is having a bad day." Siobhan added helpfully. "So, what's brought you in today?"

"Oh, I don't suppose you have a copy of *Plumbing for Dummies* in stock that I could borrow over lunch? The intake pipe from my rainwater tank burst this morning and I don't have running water until I manage to fix it." She asked hopefully.

"Nope, sorry, we don't" Siobhan pronounced confidently. "I know every book we have in stock personally, we've had a lot of time to get to know one another-–that's who I was talking to when you got here."

"Okay, then could you perhaps –" Hayden began, before being suddenly cut off by Daniel, as she recalled Siobhan explaining earlier on.

"Can you tell her what the specials in the cafe are today? No, worries, right this way ma'am." He proclaimed loudly, gently tugging her arm towards the cafe's main seating area; a.

"Hey, that's not what I was asking, excuse me," Hayden demanded, as she was being dragged away.

"I know okay, relax, she just gets set off when people try to order new books, and no offence, but you seem far too young to be attempting to handle that conversation just yet." Daniel explained as they neared the cafes' adorable vintage rescue counter. "Besides, the entire system is integrated so I can set up your order right here."

He rounded the staff side of the counter as he continued to mitigate some personal drama for his colleague, "What was the name of the book you were looking for?" he asked.

"Oh um, *Plumbing for Dummies*?" She hesitated briefly.

"Oh damn, pipes burst huh? No worries at all, if we're lucky and we usually are in here, it'll be here by the end of next week, can't really promise anything closer since we mostly rely on the trains, and you know how reliable they are." Daniel informed her.

The thought of having to go a week without a shower irritated her beyond comprehension, but it did give her the thoughts of spending the week digging out a space for a natural swimming pool...

"What's your name? I'll need it for the order," he asked, seemingly not for the first time.

Hayden snapped her attention back to the present, smiled and caught herself up on the conversation.

"Oh Gods, sorry, I dazed off, I'm Hayden Shott," she continued, giving her contact information so that they could contact her when the book arrived.

Deciding that daydreaming at the counter was a sign of her caffeine levels being blasphemously low she ordered herself a white-chocolate mocha and asked Daniel what his current favourite read was and if they had a copy she could borrow.

Taking a seat on one of the plush, blue-green loveseats she listened to Jason as he set to work, singing *A Thousand Miles by Vanessa Carlton*. The only thought that she could relate it to was as if *Terry Crews* himself was making her coffee! Looking around at the decor while listening to Jason serenade the coffee machine gave her a simple joy that made that little hallmark channel girl inside her all soft.

The main dining area was beautifully laid out with a combination of smaller and larger table configurations. With the smaller tables having tall wingback chairs and loveseats and the larger more gathering sized tables having the smaller chairs. Catering to groups of one to ten by the looks of the current set up.

The Yuletide decorations were littered across the tables. Despite the heat outside, the air conditioning kept the mood inside festive. Found forest items like dried pinecones, oak and eucalyptus leaves surrounding the battery candles, all gave the space that extra cozy feeling. So, as her coffee and book arrived she was pleasantly surprised to look up and see Jason towering over her table.

"Hi there? Hayden, right?" His deep voice booming even in its lowered state. She nodded her response, smiling enthusiastically as he continued to prattle adorably, "I've got your white-chocolate mocha and copy of *The Greek Myths by Robert Graves?* Since you're only here for morning tea, I've only brought you volume one, but there is a second if you'd like to borrow that another time or buy a copy for yourself. I've also brought you a blueberry muffin because, now I may be wrong, but I think you might have ADHD, and that would mean you likely didn't have breakfast this morning since you didn't get to have your morning shower. I've warmed it up, but Patrick really is a genius for this, which, when you think about it, makes absolutely no sense at all."

"Wait, why would that make no sense at all?" Hayden interrupted questioningly.

"Oh, because he's a poltergeist, he doesn't consume food. Can't even try any of it." Jason laughed, as he placed the plate in front of her.

Leaving her to her food and reading, Jason took himself back to the coffee machine. The first bite of the muffin was something else entirely. Somehow, Patrick the poltergeist had managed to capture exactly what every blueberry muffin should be. Buttery soft with a berry for every bite, with just a hint of cinnamon swirling through.

The coffee however had been almost unbelievable had she not ordered an iced version to take away. The true test was its versatility, one sip as she turned over the engine of her Subaru confirmed as such, **best coffee this side of the planet,** one-hundred percent.

Finally feeling as though she'd accomplished something. Despite lack of a shower for the next week, Hayden headed back home, somehow managing to stop at the supermarket on the way to buy as much bottled water as her boot would allow.

Three

The caffeine buzz was still more than comforting as she pulled back into the homestead, compiling the tasks she still had left to do after bringing in her ton and a half of bottled water.

Sanding the living room--who knew that that was the worst part of DIY after the sheer cost! Finish building the chicken trailer, and sorting something out for dinner—do I still have some of that curry in the freezer?

With red chicken curry on her mind, Hayden checked the freezer and pulled out her Tupperware placing it in her drying rack. Deciding that the sanding could wait until she had running water once more, she headed out the back door to the rusted out trailer she'd found on the property a couple of weeks earlier.

Hayden had seen a few youtube homesteaders swear by these coops on wheels, to help regreen barren land. Thinking it can't have been as hard as she imagined it would be to build for herself, Hayden had pulled the rusted out trailer through the dry sticks and thorny weeds for hours the day she'd found it. Here, just beyond her backdoor it had remained ever since.

By the time the mid-afternoon sun had forced her to run back into the coolness of her airconditioned bedroom, Hayden had managed to get most of the rusted bay off of the frame. Which thankfully seemed to still be in good enough condition to actually use. Throwing her curry into the microwave, she continued through to set her A/C and TV to the perfect temp and volume.

A little while later, Hayden had changed into fresh clothes, washed her face and was curled up in bed with her TV playing her favourite soft music with a digital fire crackling. Book in one hand, curry spoon in the other and memories of blueberries had her easing into the first truly restful sleep she had had in a long long time.

The familiar honking of her mothers' personal ringtone echoed throughout her room, shocking her into alertness as if the woman had suddenly burst into her bedroom, like she had when she was a child. Taking a moment to gather herself, she attempted to use her voice as if she had been up for a while and already had had her first cup of coffee.

"Morning Mum," she answered. Quickly glancing at the time, she realised that she had indeed slept the morning away, she continued with her safest greeting, "how were the markets this morning?"

"Good morning Darling, oh they were fine, packed as usual but we got in and got out with what we wanted. How's it been up your way? Found a job yet?" Lileth jabbed in response.

"Actually yeah I have, I get to start just after the holidays, and I'll have a store discount too which will make the renovations so much more affordable." Hayden snarked back, though Charlie never mentioned anything about a staff discount, she didn't think the lie was too excessive.

"Oh that's so wonderful to hear Darling, I'm so glad you've managed to find something stable in this economy. You're so brave for moving out into the desert all by yourself, at least your Father and I won't need to worry anymore about having to come up there to rescue you from financial ruin. We didn't want to say anything but we really don't have the money to come and help with anything if something happens."

Despite the absolute ease with which Lilleth was capable of underlying every potential compliment with the sharpest barb possible, it was more the fact that she was so happy to be breezing through any possible jabs about Hayden's new job that concerned her.

She had some other reason to call this early in the morning, what could it be? Hayden thought to herself as she listened to her mothers' cruel tone.

"Mum I've told you, I know what I'm doing out here—crazy as it may seem—but I've got this. You and Dad just focus on your health and surviving through the economic crash in the city, okay? You don't need to worry. Has anything else happened this week for you guys?" She deflected, hoping to avoid accidentally mentioning her intake pipe.

"Actually, now that you mention it, your brother has a bit of good news. He's been asked to run the Labor Party's Candidate Election in preparation for the National Election next year!" Lilleth announced.

Of course he fucking has! That sly mother-fucker would sell oil to eskimo and tell him it's gravy, just to make a dollar! Not giving a flying fuck if everyone else is screwed, including the planet, in the process! Fury and disgust coursed through her, burning like acid as it went.

"Really, that's brilliant, I'm so happy he's doing so well." The lie burnt her throat as the taste of bile washed around her mouth. Sounding as unconcerned and genuine as she had managed since answering, she thanked every God and Goddess she'd ever heard of that she had learned this one skill from her mother.

"Isn't it just?! Your brother could be chief of staff to the next Prime Minister! Someone from **our family**

would finally be working within the walls of Parliament House!" Her pride evident in her voice showed that her brilliant ability to lie had absolutely no audience today.

Lileth couldn't care less what Hayden thought, today's call was simply gloating that her eternal favourite was once again succeeding at being the apple of her eye.

"I'm glad for you Mum, really, and I'd love to stay on the phone catching up more but unfortunately I only have a few more weeks left until I start work in town, so I'd better get a move on with my renovations." Hayden replied sarcastically.

"Of course Darling, talk soon." Having gotten the grumbled response she wanted, Lileth ended the call having said the last word.

Shuddering at the thought of Paul working as chief of staff to the Prime Minister of Australia, honestly just the thought of Paul working in the same building as the Prime Minister was enough to horrify her.

Deciding that today was in fact the worst day to attempt anything at all, she shut her black-out curtains and climbed back into bed.

Four

Having well and truly slept off the feeling of slime and sweat that always filmed her skin following a call from Lilleth. One day Hayden would finally be able to tell her mother exactly what she thought. Maybe then she'd be able to stop feeling the sense of dread that always came with the honking ringtone she had set on her mothers' number.

For now though she would have to cave, it was going to be a much easier week if she simply spent a little extra money this month and paid the fee for the gym in town. At least there she'd be able to take a shower so she could get started on the renovations again.

In her delirium yesterday Hayden had thought of painting her living room the most horrendous shade of yellow. Lileth had always abhorred the colour family simply because she believed it made her look like she was yellow, like sick with liver failure. The thought, though entirely ridiculous, made her smile so brightly that she simply had to find a way to get back to work.

Any way that she could make her mother loathe coming out to visit would be worth any financial cost. Hell, that was how Hayden had wound-up buying this place, she still hadn't found a good enough reason to regret her actions either.

Feeling as though that was the best excuse and realising it was now the only reason she needed to satisfy anymore, Hayden set about planning how she wanted to set out the homestead. In the end, her runaway thought from the other day about building a natural swimming pool became a fully fleshed out idea. Along with an actual plan for how to make the chicken trailer really work for her and the realisation that maybe she needed to do a lot more research into how to do everything she needed in the easiest ways.

Naturally this called for a visit to Borrow Me Books & Cafe, before leaving she packed herself a bag to take to the gym, both workout clothes as well as an outfit for after. With the thought of Jason's mochas and whatever Patrick had cooking up in the kitchen spurring her onward, Hayden ran out the door with literally nothing to lose anymore.

The drive into town was as easy as ever, the distance becoming less and less of an issue for her as time went by. The sheer joy that Hayden got from having the window down and listening to the deafening wind racing by with the taste of mocha on her lips.

Resolving first to go to the gym, she turned left off of main street as she entered, taking her to the back entrance of the locally owned one.

The owner was nice enough to help organise her membership before starting the customary tour, letting her first use the complimentary showers. Before leaving she did a customary hour-long work-out since she was planning to finish off the sanding in the living room, which meant that Hayden could justifiably spend the entire afternoon at the bookstore researching easy to create natural swimming pools and what animals were best suited to helping re-green her near desert of a homestead in the way that those guys in Africa have been doing it.

On her way to the bookstore Hayden stopped by the hardware store and chatted to Jayne about her trials with sanding back the excess plaster from spackling earlier in the week.

"I'm just not sure what I'm doing wrong. All the tutorials say that realistically it should take more than a couple of days to sand. Did I leave too much of the plaster on the wall?" She worried, showing Jayne the photo on her phone.

Taking the phone, Jayne seemed to consider it seriously before replying.

"No, I don't think your issue is that you've left too much spackle behind. But," he began, looking up with a small mischievous smile, "is that the sandpaper and block you're using to sand the walls with?"

"Yeah, why? Isn't sandpaper just sandpaper?" Hayden replied sheepishly.

"Sorry, no. It's honestly an easy mistake to make but realistically you're going to need to start collecting some tools."

Jayne set about showing her the power tools and explaining their uses. He recommended a brand that was well known for creating more versatility for their pre-existing tools so that their customers would only need to buy an adaptation piece rather than having to buy a whole new power tool. Thinking the system was genius, she added the drill and sander to the trolley before they moved on to the paint section.

Sussing that there may be quite a bit more research in store for her later, Hayden took the opportunity to pick Jayne's brain about how to best achieve the paint scheme she wanted for her living room.

"Just out of curiosity, do I need to do anything after I've sanded it or can I just put the yellow paint on there?"

Jayne gave her a look that seemed to say *"Really?"*

But instead of saying that, he simply steered them towards the paint section and detailed everything she could possibly need to know.

"To start with you're going to need to use the shop-vac you bought last month to vacuum up all the dust that's left behind. Then, my personal suggestion for a really clear paint is to get a damp cloth and wipe that sucker down. Well, unless you're jumping on the roman-plaster revival that's going around, in which case you don't actually need to do any prep other than mixing your plaster with the paint of your choice."

"Well that sounds easy, what does it look like when it's on?" Hayden commented, looking up from the colour swatches of yellows she found Jayne already searching through his phone.

"Am I glad you asked!" He responded happily. "I've been trying to convince people to try it because it's so easy and it looks so cool."

Turning his phone Hayden was able to see the matte finishing with all the different textures adding depth wherever the light hit it.

"Oh yeah! I can see why, that'd be perfect to use with the yellow, I might even do the main mix with this yellow and get a small can of that metallic gold to swirl through at the end. It'd make the living room look like it's caught on fire every afternoon when the sun comes through!" She beamed, grinning from ear to ear.

"That's even better than what I did!" Jayne approved.

"Wait, that's your house?" She gushed in response.

"Yeah, I gave mine that deep gothic revival look. It's my wife's favourite so I wanted to impress her when we first got together. Now she has fun decorating it with found oddities." Jayne replied as he pocketed his phone.

"I guess it worked then." Hayden smiled.

They laughed as she and Jayne finished gathering the other things she would need in order to do her plan justice, and swearing to take before and after photos, she loaded her car and set off for her caffeine fix.

Five

S tepping into the store gave Hayden that same sense of awestruck wonder that she had when she first walked in a few days earlier.

Deciding that caffeine beat research, she waved at Daniel as she made her way to the cafe. As she looked over the specials board and at the array of pastries, quiches and rolls in the glass fridge next to the counter.

"Welcome back, need a hand deciding?" Jason asked as he returned with his delivery board, placing it down as he neared the register.

"You know what, I can't decide, what would you recommend?" Hayden pleaded earnestly.

"Well that would depend on what you were looking for, are you wanting something for lunch, a snack or a whole meal plan for an afternoon of grazing?" He needled, her squirmed response at his last guess brought a smile to his eyes.

"Grazing plan then? Cool, my suggestion would be to tell me what you're allergic to and I'll pass it on to Patrick, then he can have fun whipping something up and everyone always loves what he comes up with. Otherwise you'll end up eating vegan food and not many people like my mainly grains and greens diet." Jason laughed as he set about fixing the coffee machine.

"That's incredible!"

"You go ahead up to the stacks and I'll start on your first mocha, just ask Daniel to take you up and show you around. Siobhan's on break and hasn't been sleeping well." He entreated.

Noting that she had no allergies, Hayden went over to the sales counter, realising that maybe it was the bookstore that Charlie had been onto something about working here, resolving to talk to Jason at another time about it.

"Howdy," Daniel said by way of greeting.

"Howdy? Not something you hear every day outside the states. I'm alright, in desperate need of a research station. Can you help a girl out cowboy?" Hayden joked back.

"Absolutely ma'am," he chortled back in a terrible attempt at a southern drawl, "what kind of research are you doing? We'll see if we can find a booth near that, them books."

"Hmm it's a bit of a mix really, I need to have a look at how to create a natural swimming pool, but I also have a bunch of regreening and homesteading research to do. What do ya think?" she confessed.

"Oh, definitely," he stated, reverting back to his normal voice. "There's a really big research booth that a few of the students like to use for group project meetings. It's right next to the natural history stacks."

Following Daniel up the wide staircase to the right of the cafe, Hayden admired the ornately carved railing. He led her to a nook where a large booth had been built into the oddly-shaped space. Plush velvet seats surrounded a large circular table with a built-in lazy susan in its centre. As she placed her bookbag and her laptop case on the table, Daniel reached out his arm tentatively.

"Careful, the table itself also spins the entire way around, people have fallen and hit their heads when they weren't careful," he warned helpfully. "Aside from that, the bathrooms are just down that way and if you need a hand finding anything, just let us know."

"One more thing before you go," Hayden beseeched. "What's the wifi password?"

A little while later, she had her laptop open to an Australian YouTuber who had been regenerating the soil of her family's desertified cattle farm. Putting her headphones on she went searching through the stacks that seemed to span the entire central area of the second story. As she made her way back to the booth armed with several volumes about landscaping architecture and creating natural habitats, Jason was putting the tray down with her coffee and some kind of pastry.

"Perfect timing, Jason," she remarked as he turned around.

"In here? Always." He smiled. "What have you got there?"

She began telling Jason all about her sudden idea earlier in the week about creating a natural swimming pool. The more ideas she babbled, the happier he seemed to become, until at last Hayden had to ask, "do you like what I'm saying or am I just being ridiculous at this point?"

"Not crazy at all, I love what you're doing and honestly, I think more people should be doing it too. It's the best kind of filtration system for most water too, even better if you use a few smaller ones instead of dams." He agreed.

"That's brilliant! Of course, because animals love immersing themselves in water too, don't they?" She guffawed at the obviousness that most farmers seem to be overlooking.

After pointing out a few websites with some more specific information about natural pools, Jason showed Hayden where more of the complete ecosystem textbooks were.

"If you're interested in creating complete habitats for your homestead, then you might want to check out our indigenous land practices shelves. There aren't many, but we have more than most, if you hear of any that we don't have then let me know and I'll get the store a copy." He pointed to a stack of shelves a little further away before walking back towards the booth with the books he had recommended.

"Patrick will be up in a bit with your lunch, I have no idea what he's doing in there, but he seems happy," he insisted, as he retrieved his tray.

"Can I ask what this is or do I need to try it first?" Hayden asked as she picked up a buttery-looking pastry.

"I'd prefer you to try it first, but it's not a requirement," Jason suggested. She took a bite and was pleasantly surprised at the creamy filling. "You asked for my recommendation, my favourites are the pandandus-nut croissants that Patrick makes—they're gluten-free too, so everyone can enjoy them. They go great with the white chocolate mochas too."

After taking a bite, she understood what Jason had meant, a creamy, nutty and velvety smooth filling burst into her mouth. The creamy smooth texture evoked a sense of pistachio butter, but with a vanilla-nutty flavour. Subtle favours, delicate pastry and a mocha that fuelled the frenzied start to her afternoon of research.

Time passed swiftly and as the caffeine buzz from her first mocha started to wear off, a tray appeared on the lazy suzan in front of her.

"Girl, I'm gonna have to ask you to look up from that big 'ol book there and give that tired neck of yours a break, 'kay honey." Looking up from the tray, Hayden found a mostly transparent being, standing off-kilter with a hand on one hip, the other was fanning the tray in his face as if it were a hand fan. "I'm Patrick babes, but you can call me Ricki, I keep trying but no one ever does."

"Oh hey, it's nice to finally meet you. Your baking is out of this world," she confessed excitedly.

"Aw thank babes, but it's not actually out of this world, if anything it's more of this world than what's in the supermarket really. Like what you have for lunch here, Mob Taco's, everything in it was grown on Mob land. It's more local than us, aye." He explained as he indicated the tray in front of her. "You've got a stewed roo tail with a desert tomato and bulbine salsa and pepperberry hotsauce. A fried trout with salsa and desert tomato bbq sauce taco and a witchetty grub with a quandong vinaigrette."

The scene from The Lion King, where Timone and Pumba are convincing Simba to try a grub for the first time, instantly popped into her head, unsure if it was going to be more than a bite for that one.

"They sound amazing, so why Ricki?" She asked, distracting from the thought of grubs for lunch.

"Well, I like it, but no one's using it. At the moment it's either Patrick, ew, or Patty—thanks to Jason, the little asshole," Ricki gossiped. "But that's enough chatter I've got a kitchen to get back to, you better eat up them grubs aye. They'll help your neck so you can sleep tonight."

With that he became almost more transparent and headed back downstairs.

Along with her mob tacos, Ricki had brought another mocha which she happily sipped as she worked up the courage to finally try her witchetty grub taco. Honestly, if either of the first two were anything to go by then she was in for something amazing. Still unable to brave the grubs, Hayden picked up one of the volumes that Jason had recommended earlier.

Finding a relevant section on the processes of soil regeneration, she took another sip and began taking notes on her trusty legal pad. Her mocha had sat long enough that it was stone cold by the time she looked up from the book once more she caved.

In the end the grubs really weren't that bad, a crunchy and seasoned coating disguised the crunchy shell in a way she actually found appetizing. The gooey insides, while creamy and fatty, were completely overpowered by the quandong vinaigrette.

Not exactly something that Hayden would probably order off of a menu in Sydney, but at least now she wasn't as afraid of being broke as her family had always tried to encourage her to be.

As the afternoon wore on and the exhaustion from running all over town began to set in, Hayden began to pack up her things. Saving the three books she had found most useful, giving her more than a few different step by step guides on how to work with the soils and habitats that are native to the area, rather than trying to fight it.

Making her way down the ornate staircase, still focusing on one of the websites that she had brought up on her phone, Hayden almost missed Ricki as he carried a cup of what smelled seductively like another mocha.

"Is that for me or is someone else as equally addicted as I am?" she joked, interrupting his path.

"Ah well, yes, but are you heading off? 'Cos I don't mind wrapping this all up for you to take home."

At Ricki's statement, Hayden took in the rest of the plate. A plethora of smaller bowls and plates surrounded a very large mug of white chocolate mocha.

"Are you sure? This all looks and smells so good, I'd hate to leave it."

"You go settle up with Siobhan, Dan finished work a couple of hours ago, and Jason is on his way out too," he instructed.

Nodding in a way of reply, she headed over to Siobhan's usual station, finding it empty.

"I'm over here dummy," she called. "Honestly, humans have no sense of their surroundings. It's a wonder you all managed to survived childhood."

"Sorry, my head's still in a book and in the dirt. How's your day been?" Hayden coaxed.

"That's okay, you're the last customer for the day so I get to go home when Patrick is finished cleaning up the kitchen. You're not making him waste his entire dinner menu are you? He spent an hour trying to decide what to do." She stressed.

"Of course not!" Hayden cried out, confronted at the thought of hurting Ricki's feelings. "He's wrapping it all up so I can take it home and eat it there. I'm just heading off because I'm afraid I'll fall asleep on those plush couches in the research nook."

"Oh, that makes sense, I actually have fallen asleep on those couches," she said, pondering for a moment with a hand on her chin. "Actually, I'm not sure it counts as sleeping since I'd forgotten that the table spins and, uh, bumped my head a bit. Anyway, I definitely remember the comfiness of the couches when I was waking up at least."

Smiling at the way Daniel had warned her earlier, she realised that maybe it wasn't as rare a thing as it seemed it would've been. Siobhan handed her a bag with the volumes she'd selected just as Ricki was approaching them with a bag in one hand and a takeaway cup tray in the other.

"Hey, are you ready to go?" Siobhan queried sweetly, a stark contrast to the way she usually spoke.

"Soon darl, soon. I've just got the last wipe down and mop on our way out. We're fine," Ricki soothed as he neared.

"Alright now, one of these is a mocha--this one," he explained as he passed her the cup-tray, "and the other has the gravy from the Roo tail stew. In the bag I've written down reheating instructions, so it tastes perfect."

"This is incredible, thank you so much Ricki, mmm and now I can just keep reading when I get home. This has been the best afternoon. Have a good night guys." Hayden balanced the bags in her hands with the cup-tray as she made her way out of Borrow Me.

Six

D riving home was as picturesque as always, the colours that warmed the sky as the night moved in--always making her wish that she was one of those artsy people, the type who randomly pull-over to paint or sketch or just take a photo of a beautiful scene they stumble across.

Maybe one day, she mused watching the sky change from yellow, to orange and red, then deepen to pink and purple alike.

Pulling into the homestead she saw a family of short, brown kangaroos hopping along her driveway.

Okay, I really need to start carrying a camera at least! Hayden silently despaired.

Calling it a day, she left everything except her dinner and books in the car. Setting the bags down on her kitchen counter and pulling out Ricki's instructions.

Hey babes,

You're gonna throw the stew in the microwave and put the veggies in the airfryer —they'll crisp up nice that way.

The stew you'll want to chuck on for like 2 minutes but the sauce'll only take 1 so heat 'em up separately.

The veggies will only need 2 mins on 180c in the airfryer, but your dessert will need to be in for 10mins since the pastry needs its last blast, same temp. so nice and easy.

Have a great weekend love,

Ricki & Borrow Me

Following his instructions perfectly, Hayden went off to her bedroom to turn on the AC and put her books down. Washing her face and racing the microwave to put on her PJ's she picked up her lap-table and set it carefully on her bed before racing back to the kitchen.

Losing the imaginary race with the airfryer, the buzzing of its alarm echoing throughout the space, quickly joined by the microwaves' song. The cacophony of noise reached her ears painfully as she entered the small room.

"Alright already, calm down," she said out loud as she popped the microwave door open and pulled the airfryer basket from its housing.

"Can I not have the two minutes you both promised me or not?" Hayden complained as she emptied the contents of the basket into a bowl, she pulled out the stewed meat and replaced it with the sauce.

By the time she returned to the cool sanctity of her bedroom, the sun had well and truly sunk.

Placing her food down, she fetched herself a bottle of water and turned on the tv. There was nothing particularly interesting on the television—it made for great background noise though as she thumbed through the indigenous book she'd bought.

It was about the nomadic land practices of the central and south eastern peoples. Quickly becoming engrossed, she ate the incredible food—another of Ricki's genius dishes, and read.

By the time her morning alarm went off, she had almost finished the book. Turning it off, Hayden realised what had once again happened, laughing as she finished reading the book and packed up her bed. Getting a couple of hours of naptime would just take her right back to her study days, it was almost nostalgic.

Waking up a few hours later to her alarm softly singing her to alertness, brought her into stark realisation that the slick residual feeling that Hayden had felt since her mothers' phone call earlier in the week. As if between the distance, good food, company and sleep, along with a great book —cant cure anything!

Apparently it was just about finding the right place, people and books that work best for you. At least that was what she told herself as she washed her face and went in search of some home brewed caffeine.

An hour later and the sound of her new power-sander was all anyone could have heard for miles around, as Hayden worked through the last of the tougher patches on the walls of her living room. The ease with which the plaster melted off the wall, leaving behind a smooth, ready to paint surface.

Once done and with a youtube tutorial playing through her headset, she mixed the paint and ready to use plaster that Jayne had suggested, to a sample size of the ratio it described. Once she had a slick, evenly thick mixture, Hayden poured a thin drizzle of the metallic gold that she had bought as she stirred the mix very slowly to create a swirl. Then applied it across a small section of wall, hidden behind the front door. *Just in case*, Hayden said to herself as she walked back into her small kitchen.

This needs to change soon too, I can't even get more than a couple of days' groceries in this fridge and there's no room in here for a bigger one. She chided herself while fixing a much needed caffeine refill and some lunch. Her stomach grumbled approvingly, having skipped breakfast in favour of her early morning nap.

The question is, can I live with this for the summer so that I can start on the pool or can I live without the pool, so that I can knock that wall out and extend this space?

Continuing her internal debate as she ate and literally watched the Roman Plaster mixture dry on the wall. As it did, the gold flecks swirled within the gradually mattifying paint, the varying textures creating an almost still moving image that she instantly fell in love with.

One packet ramen and an episode of Good Chef, Bad Chef later and she was back to work, mixing a much larger bucket of roman plaster and adding the small amount of gold only into her paint trays to ensure the gold remained the swirls that she had achieved the first time. Quickly realising uniformity was going to be impossible, Hayden kept the paint mixing the same, but opted to apply each roll in a different angle.

Taking a large sigh of relief, her back aching from all the mixing and the bending, and the painting--just from applying the first coat—Hayden dropped onto her couch, gently falling further into the soft cushions as she leaned back to look over her work.

The gold flecks glimmered in the whirls just as she'd hoped, watching rays of the afternoon sun spread across the expanse.

The aching in her body from all the work had finally caught up with her for the day, so Hayden pulled out one of her trusty frozen meals, beef stroganoff tonight. Promptly passing out, still seated on her couch not long later.

Hayden woke to her alarm, its usual tone somewhat muffled—with her phone still jammed in her jeans pocket—and stretched. Her aches from the previous days painting now a dull throb from the awkward sleeping position.

Determined, however, to finish painting her living room at least, so that she could feel just a little more comfortable about spending time outside her bedroom. Though, having fallen asleep on the couch made her seriously consider splurging and ordering a more comfortable couch as she set about fixing her usual morning caffeine hit.

Having dismissed the idea of buying a new couch online, Hayden scrambled some eggs and then set up her first round of roman plaster for the day. Nearly giving herself reflux from practically inhaling her food, she began applying the second coat. Realising rather quickly afterwards that she may not need a third after all.

"Well, even though it was spite that made this happen, I actually love it!" Hayden admired aloud as she looked over the varying shades and textures the each element gave the whole.

A loud knocking on the front door behind her, brought her out of her reverie. Thinking that perhaps she had unwantedly somehow summoned her mother, she opened the door a crack to see who it was.

"Afternoon Darl, we're here for the BBQ." Hayden sighed in relief at Jason's pronouncement.

"What BBQ is that?" She sputtered, wondering when exactly she had mentioned one.

"That would be the one Borrow Me is throwing to welcome you to town," Dan supplied helpfully.

"And when did I agree to this?" Hayden challenged.

"Well, about that, ah, technically speaking--you didn't. I had the idea to set it up on your behalf and well, everyone said that if I paid, they'd all help." He admitted, having the decency to at least look sheepish as he continued, "it's why I left early on Friday while you were up in the stacks."

"But why? We've only met a few times, doesn't really amount to much, does it?" She faltered.

This is ridiculous, they're having a laugh at her expense, just like her brother and cousins always did.

Hayden thought to herself, as she considered the genuine expressions on their faces.

"I get why you might think that--but the truth is, in a small town like ours, especially the farming ones, we need people. People just like you, to take a chance and just move out here, for no reason other than you can work from home and still afford to live out here. The only way to really convince you to stay would be for us to do our best to be kind. Especially since the only people who have been here longer than us are the indigenous people who are still struggling. Actually while I'm on the topic--" Siobhan began.

"I think what Sis is trying to say here," Ricki said, cutting her off, before she could launch into what was probably one of her famous tirades on equality. "We want you to feel welcome here, and we want you to know that in our town, community is the only way we survive. So shut up, accept that we're here to show you some love, and take me to the cook pit so I can get these ribs and briskets on."

Embarrassed at possibly showing her conservative, city-style upbringing, Hayden stepped aside to let them all into the refreshingly cool AC.

"I'm sorry, I've just had a lot of drama with my family in the past so I tend to keep to myself for most of the time. I've never really had visitors before, so —not entirely sure how I'm going to go with other people randomly showing up." She blushingly admitted.

"Aw, see I told you we picked a good one." Dan squeaked at her concession.

"Besides, it's just us tonight –I wouldn't have let him invite the entire town to your house without your permission," Jason started, mockingly aghast with a hand over his heart. "Especially not during summer when I know you don't have a working shower or a pool."

"One more thing," she added, "I don't actually have a cook pit."

Seven

Having been told quite unanimously that the fastest and tastiest way to cook for everyone was going to be by digging out a cook pit, they all went to work –taking it in turns so that it was done fast, without overworking anyone.

"So, how long have you been living in this place for?" Siobhan asked, as they finished up digging the last part of the new cook pit to Ricki's specifications.

"Six weeks, although the first few days were a little unnerving, I hadn't actually come and seen the place before I bought it," Hayden began to explain, laughing as she recalled her own stubbornness. "I had to sleep in my car for the first week. I have never been more thrilled at having an old SUV."

"Wait, there's a motel in town, why didn't you come in?" Siobhan coaxed.

"I, uh, bought the house after I looked at the pictures online. I didn't do any of the things I know you're supposed to do like actually look at the place for one thing, or have a contractor or surveyor come and take a look to tell me how out of my depth I was." She confessed. "Basically, there wasn't a single usable bedroom, and the living room didn't have walls or a window. It was just the studs."

"Huh, that's pretty ballsy," Jason commented as he loaded another log into the pit. "How bad was it?"

"I didn't have a single room I could actually use." Hayden clarified.

"It was pure luck that I'd actually bought the storage container for the majority of the furniture I'd found around the city before I left." She said, taking a seat at the glass and green steel garden table and continued. "There's so much stuff people are either giving away or literally just leaving on the curb. It's insane, well, that —and the fact that I have basically no money."

"Didn't you have a job in the city?" Siobhan noted.

"Yeah, well no actually-–I was a PhD student for a few years and so I was technically paid for the work I did on behalf of and for my archiving professor." She blushed and looked down, trying to avoid the looks of pity.

"Okay, so what have you managed to accomplish on a budget of less than zero? Anyone wanna come get a look?" Dans' excited tone caught her attention, the whoops of conspiratorial joy echoing his.

Before she had a chance to protest they were already gone, blasting through the still open back-door. Quickly following after them, Hayden nearly bowled Ricki over as the floating entity carried a tray of freshly seasoned meat.

"Careful darl, and just for that you can pick those trays up and bring them over aye. Once we get these on the coals you can go in and catch them before they make it to your sex-toy collection. Nice hiding spot though--I almost didn't find it." Laughing, Ricki bumped her gently with his hip gently nudging her towards the kitchen, "hop to."

Ensuring she had a steady grasp on both of the bbq trays, Hayden carried them out to the back table before finally returning to the house.

Listening to the increasingly loud giggling, she made her way down the long hallway and into the master bedroom--the first rooms she'd reno'd.

"That's impossible, no one but really weird people don't have a porn collection, or a vibrator at least," Siobhan announced magnanimously.

"Oh is that right? Or did I just build a secret door to cover the spot where it all is?" Hayden replied cheekily back.

"Of course you would, bloody librarians, every time--it has to be a secret entrance here, invisible nook there." Dan lamented, "It's never just under their bed or in the sock draw."

Jason sidled over to her, from the bathroom attached, ignoring Siobhan and Dan's continued investigation to find her porn.

"Tell me you have photos from before, because that bathroom looks amazing. How on earth did you manage to find a clawfoot tub that big?" he exclaimed, awestruck.

Excited at someone loving her trash treasures, she beamed. "Actually, I heard that this really posh neighborhood in Canberra was going under development–but I did my masters at ANU, and a friend of mines' uncle lived there years before. Anyway," Hayden stopped, having become side-tracked again–*maybe I should look into that ADHD stuff*, she thought as she continued. "The point is, I paid for a storage unit while I was studying and working full-time on top of that, and when I heard about posh old neighborhoods being bought out like that. I'd go scavenging."

"I love it, is that where you're from then–the capital?" Jason pondered.

"Nah, I'm from Sydney and did my Bachelors' and PhD at UNSW there, but my mum wasn't giving me any space as I was finishing up my undergrad study. So I told her to fuck off and I went to live in Canberra at ANU for about three years." Carrying on their conversation and leaning against the wall, Hayden and Jason watched as Dan and Siobhan continued to fail at finding her porn stash.

After another ten minutes of worsening searching Dan finally called an end to the hunt. "Just show us that you have some, and that you're not a complete psychopath and we'll leave it alone."

"Fine, but I'm only showing you the porn, you're not going anywhere near my toys." Hayden agreed, pushing off the wall and making her way to the left side of her bed, and finding the right notch in the floorboard, pushed down to release the mechanism keeping the lid to her adult library closed.

Opening with a hiss, she carefully moved aside the trap-door that housed the space under the floor.

"Holy, mother of us all, was that a temperature release?" Dan nodded appreciatively.

"Of course, how else do I keep books safe? I'm a librarian." Hayden rolled her eyes.

"Oh now this is a porn collection that I can get around!" Siobhan exclaimed, after picking through several volumes.

"Where's all the pics?" Dan dismayed, scanning through the book in his hands. "Fuck this, where else have you managed to get through?"

Taking her phone back from Jason, Hayden moved towards her bedroom door.

"You coming?" She asked Siobhan looking back over shoulder.

"Soon enough, mind if I borrow a few of these–I just found one I've never even heard of. Who's Kushiel?"

Deciding to leave her to the books, Hayden followed the guys, pointing them back to the front living room from earlier.

"I finished the walls in here just this morning. Jayne from the hardware store suggested the painting method." She excitedly babbled.

"Jayne's a good kid, took him a minute, but he's come out okay." Jason nodded. "I like the gold coming through, what method did he suggest, he's been going through a bunch of them the last twelve months–he's been driving Kaylee nuts with it."

"Huh, well, this one was Roman Plaster." Hayden considered, "I really liked the way it had come out in his pictures, but I thought the gold would catch the afternoon light better and soften the yellow a bit."

"I love it, not a colour most people would use, but my uncle would love it." Dan chatted, "why'd you pick it anyway?"

"Haha, I thought it would piss my mother off the most," she laughed as she explained in full. "My mother always used to say yellow makes me look bloated and like I'm suffering from liver failure, so I figured if I painted the first room she'd walk into a colour she absolutely loathed, then she would be less likely to want to visit."

"Can't half tell what you're running away from," Ricki announced from behind her while almost entirely transparent again, causing Dan to shriek.

"Damn dude, do you really have to do that every time?" He asked, smiling.

"Don't act all innocent up in here god-boy." Ricki taunted, "Dinner is officially all in the fire, so we've got a few hours we can waste. What's good to do out here?"

Sitting back around the outdoor table in the back of the property a little while later, the fire crackled and smouldered as the logs slowly burned down. Dan had been mixing drinks all night, but, being a light weight, Hayden had thought it best to keep to her ginger beer. However, when even Ricki began indulging in them it really made her consider.

"That fire's going to need at least another log before there's enough coals to keep the cooking going until it's all ready." He declared after taking a large swig of his second.

"I'll get it," Siobhan said, still laughing from Jasons' last comment. "Besides, I'm the only one who can really tell what is respectfully able to be used. Hold this for me."

As she rose, Siobhan handed Hayden her drink. Taking a sip, she felt light, free —*happy*. She realised as she took another sip, before Jason snatched it away.

"Ah that's a no no drink for humies, Sweet Pea. You've already crossed your limit, so it's a good thing it's just us tonight," he intoned seriously.

Despite trying to keep it in, Hayden simply giggled back at him.

"Exactly." Jason smiled indulgently and returned to recounting the time when he'd bestowed the terrible nickname 'Patty' on Ricki. "I can't have been more than, maybe nine years old at the time."

"Oh don't lie, you were twenty-three and had just come back from living in New York for three months," Ricki dobbed cheekily.

"Okay, so I might have been a little older, but not twenty-three c'mon, I only went to New York once, and I was at most twenty at the time." Jason placated playfully.

"He only remembers that because he tried to bribe every bartender in the city and still couldn't get a beer," whispered Dan conspiratorially to Hayden as the poltergeist and minotaur gently argued.

"Why can't I have any of that? And why is Patrick able to drink it?" She pestered.

Rolling his eyes in response, "Because it's just meant for stronger stomachs is all. Look, humans can tolerate a lot, just not nearly the amount Old Ones' can, it's not about exclusion, it's just about safety, your safety." He relented.

"You mean like a super-strong type of alcohol?" she tried to puzzle out.

"Not exactly, it's more like drinking morphine. Like a really powerful morphine. Basically, the amount that humans can actually digest is so minute, it's practically poison," Dan revealed.

"Oh; that makes sense, thanks for watching out for me." Making a face at the way the words sounded coming out of her mouth, Hayden sat there for a moment considering in an attempt to work out why it was she felt a warm ache from within her chest at her words.

"No one has ever looked out for me before..." She stated slowly as understanding dawned on her. Feeling the prick of potential incoming tears, Hayden stood up suddenly and walked out towards where Siobhan had wandered off earlier. "I'm going to go help Siobhan. I'll be right back."

Wiping away the silent tears now running down her face, she sniffled in an attempt to dislodge the frog now stuck in her throat. Losing sense of the direction she was going, Hayden stumbled in the moonless night. Choosing to fall as she tripped over a rock rather than twisting her ankle in a bad way, she looked up at the stars as the ache in her back —now covered in dust and dirt.

Now that was a sight that could stop time, there's a reason mankind has always looked above for insight. *If this was how those old astronomers saw the night sky, it's no wonder they couldn't tear their eyes away.* She thought as the thumping ache in her back began to settle and took a moment to admire the celestial sight before her.

"Hayden, is that you?" Siobhan's rich voice called. Pushing herself up onto her elbows, Hayden raised herself above the dry clusters of grass that surrounded her and answered.

"Yeah, it's me, I just tripped over a rock."

"Oh, you okay?" She asked, concerned.

"I'm fine, fell on my ass instead of twisting my ankle." Hayden began to explain, "the boys were starting to argue so I figured I'd come see if you needed a hand.

Or hey, could you show me how to find a respectful bit of firewood?"

Siobhan offered her hand to help Hayden up, confirming as she did "Do you even know what you're asking?"

"Yes and no, no I don't know what a disrespectful piece of firewood would be exactly, or why it's considered to be disrespectful to use it as firewood. But also, yes, I know that what I'm asking you to do is to teach me both of those." Hayden replied while dusting off the back of her legs.

"You know, you're not like any other city-woman I've ever met. The country folk all tend to keep within the bounds of nature's laws, simply because their livelihoods depend on working with it rather than against." Siobhan started walking in a direction confidently, and Hayden tottering quickly after her. "I mean, don't get me wrong, I'm happy you're not like the rest, but I'm a little worried about leaving you alone out here."

"I'm not exactly alone now am I?" Hayden sarcastically replied.

Siobhan just gave her a tired mum look, an eerily accurate one, just warmer than she was used to.

After showing her how to spot fallen logs and limbs instead of forcefully broken ones, they made it back to the rear of her still half-mangled house. The conversation the boys were having completely erased her feelings as she'd left.

"What do you mean you don't do translucent? That's speciesist!" Ricki disclaimed loudly.

"I'm sorry man, but I need them to at least be twenty-five, literally be begging for it, and have a pulse." Dan informed.

"I can mimic that." Ricki's reply was quick.

"Ugh, that's disgusting dude."

"What? Ew! Please don't ever do that." Siobhan interjected, looking pale.

The taste of bile filled Haydens' throat as the image and sensation filtered through her irrational mind –instantly feeling disgust.

"How is anyone supposed to eat now, Ricki?" She lamented.

Eight

Finding out that the reason Ricki was usually confined to the kitchen wasn't because he was a poltergeist, but because he had the oddest sense of humour that made him almost impossible to eat around made for an unexpected but hilarious turn of events. Apparently this was more of a habit than a spur of the moment thing, since he was destined to make the best food any being could ever dream up—he thought the funniest thing in the world was making people feel so sick that they couldn't stomach eating it anyway.

Siobhan had noted that it had been the reason she had run from the table earlier —not wanting to spoil the brisket. The rest of the evening became more focussed on what kinds of renovations Hayden had left already planned, in a group effort to steer the conversation away from Ricki's sick perversion.

"Didn't you say the other day you were researching natural swimming pools?" Jason began loudly, as Dan stood—looking a little green, to take Ricki back to the kitchen to start on all the sides.

"Um yeah, I took your advice actually and stayed up all night Friday reading a book I picked up on the nomadic practices of the traditional aboriginal custodians." Hayden beamed, thrilled at the academic topic.

"Oh yeah? That's fantastic," Siobhan praised, looking impressed.

"Brilliant, was it from a Tribe near here?" Jason probed, smiling.

"No, unfortunately not, but it is a place to start." She considered, "at least I think I might be forming some kind of idea. I'm pretty much just doing all of this by vibes. Is that bad?"

"Nah, can't be that bad--think about it, if more humans did the vibes thing like this than we'd probably have less nutters running the government." Cackling, Siobhan took a swig of her drink.

"Oh I know, have you seen that dork they have running the face of social media for labor at the moment —such a twat." Jason laughed.

Thinking of her brother, Hayden joined in the laughter imagining Paul trying to sound like he had half a brain.

"Please tell me you have clips you can show me." She begged.

"Sure, here." Jason passed her his phone and she tapped the screen. The idiot they were discussing was indeed her big bro Paulie. She smiled mischievously as she handed the phone back.

"That's my brother," she deadpanned.

For a moment they continued to laugh harder, as if she were joking. When she didn't join in, they exchanged concerned looks.

"No, sweet girl, say it isn't so," Siobhan pleaded.

"Sorry, can't. Paul Mastiff is in fact my older brother," she announced soberly. "But, thankfully, it's only biologically." Her smile broke before she could keep going, "And, the doctors are hopeful I can make a full recovery."

"Aye, that's the way sis!" Jason whooped, Siobhan whistling and cheering along. The commotion drew Ricki and dan back outside, trays laden with wood in their arms.

"What's all this then?" Ricki asked as he placed a tray on the table.

"Oh well, there's good news and bad news," Siobhan began. "Unfortunately our dear sweet Hayden here, is the younger sibling of the infamous twat and brown-noser, Paul Mastiff."

Ricki and Dan exchanged severe looks as they resumed their seats.

"Not quite what I was expecting, I'll be honest." Ricki admitted, "you look nothing like a dog. I mean, I have no idea who they're talking about but I'm assuming Mastiff comes from the dog breed, right?"

Laughing back, Hayden attempted to push him, only to feel nothing but air as her hand waved right through. Laughing at her failed attempt, he sat back in his seat.

"So what's the good news then, since being related to the twit trying to get that dumbass into office again, must really suck. I can make you an alcoholic version of that if you want?' Dan asked by way of reply.

"Oh, the good news is, she moved out here on her doctors advice, and they're confident she'll make a full recovery." Jason finished as he stood and picked up the long shovel.

Taking the hot coals out of the fire was hot work, though somehow Jason managed it with an ease only someone who's burnt themselves on a streaming espresso machine can do.

Conversation shifted back to the safety of her renovations, a little safety topic for being around both Ricki and food. Between the company, food and honest kindness, Hayden was hard-put to find a reason to be upset with Dan's surprise BBQ.

Monday morning dawned, and with it a revitalised and determined Hayden. Making a promise to herself, she took note of all of the advice she had received the night before from the bookstore team.

Most of it basically telling her to look for areas that have signs of already having been an old waterbed, well that and to pretty much only use native plants around the main water sources.

By the end of dinner Jason, Siobhan and Ricki had left her a list of things to do and signs to watch out for. So, as she set out with her physical map of the property, along with the satellite GPS that Siobhan had left for her to use.

"Seriously, you mark everything out perfectly, and then double check it on Friday, then bring it back to the bookstore. Your ridiculously new book should be there by then. Although, at least you'll have a working shower again," Siobhan had teased as she passed it to her.

Remembering the conversation, Hayden smiled and walked out her backdoor intent on finally learning every single inch of the property she now called home.

Once you've got it all set up, you're going to have to give this place a name. She reminded herself, walking around the remnants of last nights' fire in the cook pit.

Heading straight towards the southernmost border of the mostly desertified twenty-acre property. Marking each permanent and major landscape feature as she went. By the time she made it to the border that she had been told by the council was entirely enclosed, was , however, missing at least the center part of the southern fence. Including any posts, which the supposed thieves would have had to fill in, in order to lend the land agents any sense of benefit of doubt.

*Ugh, this is **not** the expense I needed right now.* Choosing instead to hope that it was merely a matter of reinstalling some posts and fencing along one side, Hayden continued along the path indicated on the map given to her by the land agent when she picked up the paperwork.

Rather than giving up entirely though, Hayden marked out everything, moving as many of the larger rocks as she could into what she had assumed was the approximate corner.

The sun nearing its peak and the intense Australian heat, forced an end for her morning of discovery, just not quite what she had hoped to discover. With still no signs of where to realistically, start digging and clearing out a space for the natural swimming pool she had planned.

Thinking it would be a wasted opportunity to head back a different way, she walked back towards the house along where the eastern fence should be.

As she did, Hayden managed to stumble across what appeared to be the entrance to a burrow of some kind. Looking around as she pulled her phone from her pocket, she searched for as many animal signs. Hoping to show Siobhan later when she went to town—*another necessary trip to use the showers at the gym, so obviously a caffeine stop at Borrow Me was necessary,* she thought to herself as she worked her way back to the house.

Making it back with relative ease on this route, Hayden took care to remember it as she gathered herself an extra set of clothes for her gym bag.

On the plus side though, she thought to herself, *at least I don't have to do any cardio today.* Thanking the spur of the moment cross-country hike, she ambled her way into the beat-up SUV and headed down the Blacktop Highway into town.

Despite still stinking from all the paint, plaster, ash, sweat and dirt, the long drive into town was as gorgeous as ever. More-so really, given her recent reading material. Her latest research into aboriginal land practices have seemed to really give her a better sense of the beauty within the Australian Outback.

All the while smiling at the fact that her pain-in-the-ass brother, mother and every other crazed city slickers' had absolutely no idea what it was they were missing out on.

Hayden drove past fields, and fields of wheat farms scattered between half-desertified cattle stations, wondering all the while if there was any real hope at whether or not her neighbors were going to be able to afford to celebrate Yule this year. Growing increasingly concerned as she neared the edge of the town.

Later as she was working out, thoughts of how she could help the local farmers and townsfolk celebrate the yuletide season continued to plague her, so by the time she was actually smelling human once more, Hayden had formed the beginnings of an idea, it would however, mean that she needed to get to her caffeine asap!

Rounding the final corner Hayden was surprised to see the amount of cars parked out front. Upon entering the store though, her questions were quickly answered. It seemed as though the town was holding a meeting in the cafe space of the bookstore.

Quietly shuffling over to the Borrow Me counter where Siobhan sat at her station listening to the discussion happening across the way.

"Hey, I didn't expect to see you until the end of the week?" She whispered as Hayden drew nearer.

"Had to come into town anyway to use the shower at the gym. I figured I'd come in to check on the book while picking up some coffee." She clarified in a hoarse whisper, after taking a quick sip from her drink-bottle she asked, "what's going on? Town Meeting?"

"Not really, it's just about the Yule Markets we have every year—it's usually run by the old owner of the shop." Siobhan began to explain.

"He passed away about eighteen months ago, but he had a pretty sizable trust –never said how he got the money, but he left it all to the shop. To keep it going so that the town would always have access to knowledge, and so that there would always be a place for The Old Ones, like us —" indicating the others who worked in the store, as she continued. "A place to exist within the world of humans."

Hayden stood there, staring at a book bound in green leather on the shelf, over Siobhan's shoulder—thinking about how incredible it was that she had never heard of this place before.

"Why did he do that?" She pondered aloud. Startled by the sound of her own drifting voice, Hayden quickly looked to the Dryad standing before her and seeing the fury beginning to seep into her nut-brown eyes she corrected profusely, "not in a why would someone do that kind of way--just a that's awesome but I wonder if there was more to it than just making sure you and the others had somewhere safe."

Watching as the anger turned to hurt, Siobhan looked away briefly, "I don't know, he wasn't from around here. He moved out here from the city about thirty or forty years ago now, he just said 'I wanna help.'"

Catching her eye once more, she continued "I've lost people I loved, because there wasn't somewhere that they could go, and this place saved me—this town did. I have no idea what we're going to do, but no one can seem to come up with anything that doesn't involve costing the town more than anyone can afford."

Looking back over to the cafe space, Hayden saw the looks of worry, as if everyone had been depending on this one thing to make the frustrations of the last farming year disappear for just the smallest of moments.

"I think I might have an idea, but I'm not sure that they'd think it is. Can I have a bit of help?" Turning back to Siobhan, she began to detail the gist of what she had come up with during her workout earlier. Expecting a different reaction entirely, Hayden's heart warmed at the hope seeming to edge its way into Siobhan's face.

"There's a few things that you'd need to think about first, but I'll help. Go grab a chair and order your coffee while you have a chance. The moment they go on break it'll be an hour before you get another shot."

Getting a hurried hello from Daniel as he took her order —Jason, already looking a little pale from the stress he was under, missed her as she ducked through the crowd picking up an unoccupied seat as Hayden returned to the counter with Siobhan.

"You know this would take literal years, right?" Indicating the new stack of cloth-bound volumes now resting on the bench, Siobhan asked solemnly. "You can't just start doing this and then fuck off back to Mummy, and Daddy when things get too hard."

"I want to make this place my home, I don't care how long it takes, just as long as we can be sure it will work," Hayden replied simply as she slouched onto the counter. "I just wanna help too."

"I'm not sure you really have it in you," Siobhan dismissed, adding with a sigh, "no offence."

Scrunching up her face, Hayden took just a little offence at the perceived slight, until thoughts of what returning to the city would look like ran through her mind. Shuddering at the thought of once again being trapped in her mothers' house, Hayden jerked upright.

"I get it, I know plenty of city people--my family included—who are exactly how you think they are, but I promise you I'm not like that," she pleaded earnestly. "Besides, the only thing left for me in the city is a lifetime of being my brothers' lapdog."

"Good, because there's only one way to get everyone in town to listen to you, and that's by knowing everyone." Siobhan smirked, the fire in her eyes setting Haydens' stomach drop into nothingness.

"I have a volunteer to organise it! She's literally got a PhD in organising–she'll be perfect!" She announced loudly to everyone over at the cafe'.

Hayden felt the blood drain from her face as the entire room turned to face them. Giving a weak smile, she lifted her hand slightly in a feeble attempt at waving. "Uh, hi?"

Turning back to face Siobhan widening her eyes, silently begging for help. Siobhan just shook her head, smiling as the room grew painfully quiet. Facing the now staring crowd, she took a steadying breath and waved once more. *Better than the last at least,* she thought to herself.

"Hi, sorry, I'm Hayden–new in town, I bought the old shack down on Old Blacktop Road?" Hayden attempted to supply helpfully as she continued, "I do technically have a PhD in archiving –which is a kind of organising I suppose. In any case, I do think I might be able to help. Though I'm not sure whether a sales market in the usual sense would really work here. At least not while the economy is so crazy.."

A few people nodded agreeably, others were evidently not happy with her suggestion, but they did begin to discuss it. As the hour drew by, her suggestion was debated, mostly between the towns' agricultural labor union rep, Tony, as Jason had told her when he'd brought over her mocha, and Elenore, the owner of a local jewelry store. By the time they'd all called lunch, and an end to the meeting, the majority had agreed to her suggested alternative.

Unfortunately the vote to make Hayden in charge of ensuring it all went ahead smoothly, did wind up being eight against three. Ricki's vote, despite his enthusiasm and subtle threatening, however, didn't count, nor did Dan's. According to Siobhan it was because they had successfully weaselled their ways into being the deejays at a community event a few years' prior and no one had let them even vote for anything since.

Nine

T he rest of the afternoon was spent deep in conversation—mostly with the towns' small council and the Borrow Me staff. As Hayden helped clean up the cafe when the meeting was finally called to an end. At which point Hayden was left in charge, and almost no one thought she was going to be able to pull this off without draining her own bank account in the process.

"What was it that Cameron meant?" she asked the others, setting the spray cleaner onto one of the tables, and wiping it down.

"When?" Jason asked before letting steam out of the frother.

"About the gift-making stations...when he said if I could pull that off, I'd be voted Queen of Yule?" she clarified.

"Oh yeah, don't worry, you won't have to do a parade or anything, but we may ask for you to honour us all with a Queenly song," Dan joked back, dancing a little jig behind the sales counter as he closed out the till.

"Haha, nah, he was talking about Kath and Elle. They've hated each other since high-school, no-one's been able to get them to even be on the same street, ever since some big blow up over class-some-thing-or-other," Siobhan replied with a shrug, lifting a tray of dirty dishes as she did.

Turning to Jason, Hayden pleaded, "have I really shot myself in the foot with this?"

"No Darl, I don't think so—well you might be asking for a bit much with Kath and Elle. But you're heading in the right direction with the Fair." he amended, "look, there's just a lot of bad blood there and I don't think anyone but those two know what their issue really is. What I do know though, is that a lot of people have tried to stick their noses into it and have been slapped for the attempt. I also know that they both love this town. If you keep it all to that without trying to pry into what's going on between them, you might actually get somewhere."

With a shrug Jason went back to cleaning the espresso machine, with a tenderness most artists would give to a prized piece of canvas. Thinking about his suggestion, Hayden went back to wiping off the tables while silently compiling a to-do list in her head.

As Siobhan returned to collect the last of the dishes for Patrick, Hayden realised with a jerk—that despite the now looming pile of errands she would need to run, she still had absolutely no idea where anyone lived.

"Would anyone be able to help me write out a list of people I'll need to talk with about all this? And maybe help me with their addresses?" Hayden asked, feeling dismayed.

"Of course!" Siobhan replied enthusiastically. Looking up from the tray laden with dishes, Siobhan finally caught sight of the anxiety that had been plaguing Hayden all afternoon.

"I'll even drive out with you, be there the whole time if you want. I wasn't going to throw you in the deep end without jumping in myself, that way I can help you make it to the finish line." She attempted to clear the air, "I like you, you're not what I expected–a humie from the city, and all, but you don't suck. That means a lot to me, okay?"

"Not that she wouldn't have done the exact same thing if she didn't like you." Dan joked sarcastically as he closed out the sales counter, causing Jason to make the loudest snort Hayden had ever heard as he attempted to hold back his laughter.

Picking up a cushion from a booth, Siobhan joined in the laughter. "Ouch!" She mocked, as she threw the cushion across, frisbee style. Whizzing past Daniel and knocking a few volumes off of the shelves behind him. "I mean, true, but rude to say asshole!"

It was becoming a thing for her, being around other people, talking to them and everything. It had never been something that she was encouraged to do. Not by her colleagues at the university—most archivists and librarians were the same as her though. It was the same for her classmates at school though, and her family at home before that. It was like she was always standing outside, any time she tried to reach out, her hand would be bitten off.

But this? This was different, this was new—it was terrifying as hell. Somehow though, Hayden thought as she drove home, *it was an excited kind of scary—as if she really was looking forward to all the scary parts. Or maybe it was just the fact that as terrifying as Siobhan was, she knew she wasn't going to have to face doing everything on her own again. Either way,* internally monologuing as she pulled up to her house, *it seems like I might actually have friends.*

A brief thought about researching how to do public speaking without stuttering or crying crossed her mind as she climbed out of the car—but then the thought of literally anyone ever finding out terrified her enough to quickly dismiss the entire thought.

Simmering the sauce for the pasta dish that Ricki had forced her to accept, she thought about what they might actually need to consider while they were talking to everyone. Deciding it might be better to print out some question sheets, she pulled her laptop from its case, and set it next to the stove.

When the pasta had been stirred into the sauce for a minute she plated up, and pulled over a stool. Opened her favourite word processor, and began to note everything she wanted to ask.

Waking up to Siobhan banging on her door however, was not what Hayden had thought support sounded like.

"What time is it?" She asked sleepily, as she poured boiling water into the coffee press.

"Six...why?" Siobhan impatiently replied.

"Why are you here at six o'clock in the morning? Who goes visiting people at six o'clock in the morning?" Hayden muttered. The irritation and exhaustion from the last few weeks finally setting in.

"Uh, farmers, and people who have jobs?" Her sarcastic reply was accompanied by the universal 'duh' face.

Recalling the conversation they had shared after locking up the store last night, Hayden stood still. Holding the coffee pot in one hand, and the sugar in the other, she turned to face Siobhan.

"Fuck, I am so sorry, I swear—I got side-tracked last night." She desperately began to explain, "I just thought today and later on, it would be better to keep a record of everyone who participates, and how they do, but I fell asleep on the bench."

"It's okay, I don't care that you fell asleep. I'm here because the only chance we have of catching all the farmers is to get them while they're at home having breakfast, after their dawn and pre-dawn chores," Siobhan stated.

"I know, and that's exactly what you told me last night, I just forgot for a second and I snapped—I'm so sorry." Hayden apologised again.

"Can you please stop saying that? You're fine honestly, we just need to get a move on—the coffee I get, but can we get this shit to go please?" Siobhan hurried.

Finally getting a move on with her usual morning routine, half an hour later they were in Siobhan's biodiesel ute and on their way to the first stop.

"So, did you at least finish the question-thingy?" Siobhan asked as they were driving along the highway.

"Mostly, I think that some questions will really only be for some of the people we talk to but there's room to add more too. I figured this would make things simpler for next year too if we actually manage to pull this off." Hayden prattled.

"If you can get Elle and Kath to work together, then I don't see a reason you wouldn't be able to chair the event next year too."

Hayden stiffened at the casual reply. The thought of running an event on an annual basis was off-putting in the least.

"Nah, I don't think so. I'd love to see what someone else could bring to it instead though. I don't mind doing the work of setting up something sustainable, but I'm not sure it's something I could do every year," she carefully responded.

"Last night I just got a little stressed at how much I don't know about the people from 'round here, and wanted to get the questionnaire ready for today. I just lost track of time while I was trying to think about what to ask. I'm an archivist, not an anthropologist—I don't know the stuff, I just organize it," Hayden laughed.

"I get that, but it might take a few years for it to actually become sustainable—think about the fact that you're dealing with people, who have lives. The whole reason you had to come up with this alternate plan for what we can do, is because life just happens." Siobhan explained slowly, "I'm just saying you might want to consider trying not to burn yourself out by trying to get everything done, all at once."

Feeling as though she was being scolded for attempting to rush it all into existence, Hayden sat quietly staring out the window at the landscape rushing past.

"What I'm trying to say is; you don't have to do this all on your own, you know." Siobhan's usually gruff voice became a softer tone. "If you'd told me last night that this was something that was stressing you out, you could have come over to my place—we could have worked on it together and probably finished it faster and with way less stress."

"Oh," Hayden replied simply. Catching Siobhan's concerned look from the corner of her eye.

"From now on, you don't need to rush to get everything done. No one is going to be upset if it isn't perfect, that I can promise you," she finished before quickly changing the topic. "Why don't you tell me what you have so far, and we can see if we can finish it off before we get to the Browns' house? We're only about fifteen minutes away, but I think we can finish it."

Hayden nodded, smiling, and happily retrieved her laptop from her bag. Siobhan was right, they finished off the questionnaire quickly enough that she was still able to give Hayden the run-down of the Browns' family, who were the only remaining cattle station managing to turn a profit in the area.

As it turned out Mrs Brown was actually the local school Principle, not out of her need, but simply the towns'. Meanwhile, Mr Brown—or Terry as everyone insisted she call him, had been the station master at Roseneath ever since his father had bought the property in the late 1980's. The beautifully green and luscious paddocks bordering the long driveway were lined with what appeared to be thorny bushes, and bunches of different fruit trees.

"Do you think you could do the majority of the talking this time? I'm just not sure that being a city-chick is going to work in my favour here." Hayden softly begged as they approached the door.

"If you're sure I can, but if you feel up for it, you should jump in. I think you'll like Polly, she's been through it a bit, but she's the strongest humie I've ever met." Siobhan offered kindly.

The warm, dark eyes that greeted them were among the softest that Hayden had ever seen look her way before. Instantly putting her at ease, though Hayden could still barely speak through the entire thing—she felt calm, and safe, and simply welcome.

"You sure you don't want a cup of tea, love?" Polly asked once more as they sat on the wrap-around-porch watching as the sun rose above the horizon.

"I'm sure, honestly, coffee is the only thing that helps my breakfast settle, and my brain work." Hayden joked again. Turning to Siobhan and silently begging her for help did absolutely nothing.

"She's not joking Polly, you should see the cafe sales—Hayden here is the one currently keeping the store open with all the mochas she drinks." Siobhan smiled as she sipped her tea.

Returning her smile, Hayden took a bite out of the English muffin, laden with the blackberry jam that Polly had made from scratch. It was her second so far, but with still no sign of Terry, Hayden became worried about needing to get on with the pitch.

"Polly, this blackberry jam is incredible—do you grow them here yourself?" She asked, curiosity winning out over logic.

"Mhmm, we have blackberries, raspberries and acacia trees lining all our paddocks—it doesn't stop the cows from getting out, but it'll deter them better than the electric fences do. The jams are a happy side effect, though it can be a bit of trouble harvesting them all." Polly replied.

"Siobhan told me that you're the local teacher too, where do you find the time?" She awed.

"Stop it, honestly, the jam gets made once—maybe twice per fruiting season. What we get is what we get, and what we don't collect from the bushes, the birds and wildlife love. It's a cheap way of stopping the cattle from wandering about, and as long as we move the cows once a week, they don't try to brave the thickets." Polly laughed.

"Don't sell yourself short Sis, you're the first black woman to be Principle here—that's no small thing. Plus, your husbands' family were here for thousands of years before that, you're more important in this town than you're giving yourself credit for." Siobhan praised.

"Terry's mob might be from around here, but all I am is mostly white with a little coffee thrown in to give the cream a little tan. I was a teacher before I moved out here, and I told Terry that unless there was a job for me outside this property, I was going to go insane. Realistically, I'm doing it all for me." She minimized before attempting to distract, "what was it that you two wanted to talk about? Something to do with the Yule Markets right?"

"Yes, actually, we were wondering how you would feel about turning the market into a fair instead?" asked Hayden.

"I'm not sure I understand your meaning. Are we not getting a stall at the markets this year or something?" Polly panicked.

"No, nothing like that—you can still have a stall if you want, but what we were hoping to organise was a Yule-Day celebration for the community. Where everyone comes into town for lunch and gift-making activities, we're hoping to make it completely free for everyone to attend." explained Siobhan quickly.

"I don't see how our council could afford to do something like that." she said, perplexed.

"We also want everyone who would normally have a stall, to still have one—but cap the prices of what you would normally have with you, so the families who usually struggle on the week the shops are closed, can have affordable food too." Hayden continued.

An hour later they were piling back into the car, Polly still wasn't convinced that it would work well enough to pay for the following year. Confirming though, that she would talk to Terry about everything—they waved Polly goodbye and set back off along the highway.

"Well, that went well." Hayden started sarcastically, "she thinks we're idiots for trying this."

"No she doesn't, she thinks that shit's expensive and that the town is broke and desperate. Which is accurate, because we are absolutely both of those." she placated once more before turning the ute down another empty highway.

"There's no sign out here, and you don't have GPS—how in the world do you know where you are right now." Hayden noted aloud. "Maybe, how many more of these have we got left to go today?"

"Nine."

"Nine?!" Hayden responded in despair, "I'm not sure I can do another nine of these."

"Well, since I'm pretty sure you want to be able to have more than just steaks and beef sausages at the Fair—you're gonna have to suck it up." she replied in an upbeat tone.

Ten

"Too much driving." She stated, for the fourth time since sitting down in the cafe.

"It was not that bad." Siobhan reiterated once more.

"I don't know, you're the one that was driving right?" Dan asked, winking at Hayden's nod, that Siobhan had been driving. "Then I don't blame you one bit—there's a reason we carpool with Jason, you know."

"Fucking asshole, you know damned well that I'm a fantastic driver—you're just still pissy about that one time I made you spill your drink." she shrilled back.

"I didn't spill it—it came back up my throat because you were speeding around a mountain on a road that had a sheer cliff off the side." he gulped, turning more olive by the second.

"Oh boo-hoo you big baby." Siobhan called, before whispering conspiratorially to Hayden, "he's conveniently leaving out the part where the night before, we had gone on a midnight drive and he'd attempted to scare the bejesus out of me. Obviously it didn't work so the next morning I woke him up at five am, and then took him out on a drive of my own."

"And do these types of drives happen often?" Hayden asked through bursts of laughter.

"Well, not nearly as much, but we do try to get a drive in every six months or so. Life and shit get in the way, but that's normal right?" A sharp bite of pain seemed to edge her voice as she answered, one that was instantly recognised in Hayden, causing a part of her that she would normally dismiss, ache in an echoed back.

"Yeah, well, I think so anyway—I um, wouldn't really know first hand to be honest." It almost broke her, offering that olive branch to Siobhan, the one that had been so damaged by others.

"I wish someone could explain it. How to let it happen without—ugh, I don't even know." Siobhan choked quietly, the others working obliviously around them.

"Without feeling left behind?" volunteered Hayden gently.

Looking up from the table, recognition shone in her eyes, "you too?"

"Yeah, that's why I started hiding in libraries in the first place. They became the known, the safe—really the only place that I could avoid all the cruelty that people seem to enjoy doling out." she admitted quietly.

"Me too, that's what this place is for me. I love it—but, this isn't what I wanted for myself." Siobhan disclosed in a hoarse whisper. "I used to be so different. I tried to be like my mum but, people were just horrible—I admit I was different, I did weird things, I knew too much, and realistically I was very loudly opinionated. Other kids hated that."

"I get that, kids can suck sometimes—especially when you're one too," she agreed.

"I thought I was going to be so cool, you know. I thought that all those mob folks on the tv would be really happy with someone fighting for them, but now, I can barely deal with the people here some days. How could I fight for anyone if I can't even fight for myself, let alone push myself to go back to school?" Siobhan divulged reluctantly, as she continued.

"What were you going to do?" Hayden softly coaxed.

"I was going to change the world," she announced scornfully, "I was going to become a lawyer and fight for indigenous rights all over Australia, you know, like the lawyers who helped Mabo back in the 90's did."

Wonder and amazement coursed through Hayden at the thought of her friend, becoming an indigenous rights' lawyer. She smiled profusely as she gushed over the thought. "Oh my Gods! That would be perfect for you!"

"Sure, except for the part that I can't stand people—well not that you count as people anymore. You're too much like us, to be called one of them." Siobhan praised.

"Thanks, seriously—I wish I had the power that you guys do, but, just being here and being friends with you guys. For the first time, I actually feel like I'm right where I'm supposed to be." raved Hayden.

"What power? I'm not sure if you've noticed this, but we don't actually have any power at all. We have innate skills—but nothing that amounts to anything more than parlor tricks." Siobhan scoffed back as she took a sip of her now iced latte.

Hayden looked at the now empty mug before her, attempting to decide whether or not the extra caffeine would impede her sleep tonight. She turned to Siobhan once more as she picked up the cup, and stood.

"I said power, not magic Siobhan. Your power comes from the knowledge you bare. I'm an archivist, remember? The most powerful thing in the world is knowledge—you and all the other Indigenous Peoples' of this world have more knowledge in your little finger than every single politician put together." Hayden proclaimed before returning to the cafe counter and organizing a refill with Jason.

"Hey, how's the plans coming along?" he asked as he finished up another customers' order.

"I'm not sure to be honest. I met every farmers' wife in town today, and I still have no idea whether anyone is actually going to turn up. How do people do this?" she asked.

"What do you mean?"

"I mean, how does anyone run these things? There is nothing stopping any of the people I spoke to today from ending the whole event. What have I done?" Hayden fretted, biting her lip between outbursts.

"Well, it starts by trusting that they want to see you succeed, and then by giving them the time to show you that." The depth of terror that now filled her was palpable—so much so that Jason began whistling and singing a Bob Marley song as he returned to making coffee.

She stood in that same fear-ridden state, listening to Jason's version of *'Don't worry, be happy'*, until her coffee was ready. Waving the mug of mocha beneath her nose, Jason startled her back into reality.

"Hey, are you okay?" he asked, concern lining his magnificent face.

"Yeah, I'm just not great at trusting people to do the right thing, for the right reasons rather than selfish ones." She huffed back, the familiar exhaustion of interacting with others settling in.

"Oh believe me, I get that. But you'll never meet decent people if you don't do the decent thing first, and give the people you don't know the benefit of doubt." He explained, his tone soothing the tendrils of anxiety webbing their way through her. "I know how hard it is to trust that random people who don't know you, aren't trying to be rude, or cruel, or dismissive. But you'll never know any different, if you don't give them the chance to show you their good side first."

Remembering the fact that she was talking to a man who had the face of a bovine, her anxiety took a pause. Looking into his warm dark eyes, she took a steadying breath.

"What if I don't pull this off? If one farmer chooses not to participate or even donate, this whole thing is going to fall apart. What am I doing?"

"You're showing them all that it doesn't matter whether or not it fails, you're showing them that you are willing to trust that they will come through, even if they don't trust themselves." Tears filled Haydens' eyes, threatening to fall as he continued, "and if the entire event does fall apart because someone pulls out, it's okay. No-one is going to be upset because until last week—everyone in town assumed it just wasn't happening again. So if it doesn't happen, that's okay, it just means that we have a great head start on planning for next year."

A sob softly escaped as she attempted to respond, placing a hand across her lips, Hayden simply nodded. Siobhan's' brief comment that morning made a little more sense now.

"Good, because while I am interested to see how your Fair turns out—I for one think you'll pull it all off, I was actually asking about your renovations. Have you decided whether to do the pool or the kitchen next?" Jason clarified.

"Oh, um." Hayden took a sip of the mocha, letting the familiar warmth wash away the slight embarrassment coursing through her. "I'll be honest, I haven't actually thought about it in a few days."

Jason took one of the empty seats at the booth, Dan had since returned, and was chatting away with Siobhan. Thinking about the tracks that had brought her into the store the other day, Hayden took the opportunity to get their opinions as the light outside began to dim. None of them could really tell, apparently Hayden had managed to snap a shot of about four different species of burrowing animals.

As they locked up the store Jason offered to come out to the homestead on his day off later in the week to help start the next reno project and check out the burrow. After first confirming with Daniel when they were going to tackle convincing the artists and crafters for that coming Friday, she and Jason organised for him to take Thursday off. The pair switched shifts to accommodate her desire not to leave the house for a few days, and as she finally fell into her bed instead of sleeping, she cried.

All those years of being pushed and poked, screamed at and bullied. By the people she thought were friends, people at school, her supposed family. In all her years, no one had ever been this patient with her. The overwhelming waves of emotion poured out again, and again, as the years of aching began to work its way out.

Eleven

Not exactly what most people would consider to be a particularly restful and healing evening, and yet the catharsis she received from literally letting all her pain and emotion pour out was unmistakable. It made even more striking against the phone call she had with her mother later the following morning.

"Oh I am so glad you picked up Sweetheart, I have brilliant news!" Lilleth exclaimed as soon as the line connected.

"Morning to you too." Hayden bit back, "what's this excellent news?"

"Paul has decided to forgive you for that little slip-up a few years ago—and is giving you the position of his personal assistant!" She egotistically declared.

"What?!" Hayden demanded. "He forgives me? Are you seriously fucking with me right now? After everything he put me through last time, why in the world would you think that I would want to work for him again?"

"Hayden, correct me if I'm wrong but, was it not you who uploaded that video of him to YouTube two years ago?" her mother cooly replied.

"Yes"

"And was that video not entirely responsible for him losing his job?"

"Also yes."

"Then why would you be the one that deserves an apology Hayden–you're being selfish. Right now your brother is perfectly positioned to become the next deputy Prime Minister and quite possibly the actual Prime Minister after that, despite your attempt at destroying his career." Lilleth scolded.

"Um, because he was stealing money from tax-payers! Literally! And the fucker tried to force me to go to prison for him, just so that he could do exactly what he's doing right now." Hayden scrunched her face in amazement at the complete lack of accountability Paul constantly received from everyone around him.

"Oh please, you would have been perfectly fine, besides the charges were dismissed so I don't see what you're complaining about. Taking the position would be brilliant for your career and his—it'll show the country that despite the events of a few years ago, even you trust him. Plus having a job means that you can finally come back home." her mother dismissed.

Taking a deep sigh to steady herself before replying evenly, "Mum, I love you, but you have to stop. I'm not coming back to the city—being out here isn't just about work, but there is absolutely no fucking way I am ever going to work with, for or near Paul again."

There was silence on the phone, long enough that she actually had to check that the line was still connected. Until the sound of her mothers' tell-tale deep breath.

"Fine, if you truly think that you know what's best then by all means—do as you will. But don't come crying to me when it all falls apart, and since everything seems to be going so well out there for you, why don't we make the long trek out there to see what you've done instead of forcing you to sit in traffic for hours this Yule?" Lilleth used her 'I-know-better-bitch' voice—the exact same one that had made her beg her grandmother for a place to sleep when she had finished her degree.

Her mother continued to speak, despite the rage Hayden was attempting to internalise, "Yes? excellent, Yule-Lunch at 1pm, I'll be sure to let everyone know that we're all invited to your house."

The bitch hung up before Hayden had managed to verbalise her fury in a scream.

"Fucking, bitch! I don't want you or any of your fucking minions near my home! I don't want any of you assholes ruining my town!" she yelled to no one.

An hour later, she was about two feet into the hole she had randomly begun digging, in order to avoid breaking more walls in her house. Still thinking over the frustrations that her family caused, and how different they were to nearly everyone she had met since leaving the city.

Tears fell as she slammed her shovel back into the ground. *Why?* She thought to herself, *why does she do this? What harm am I doing to them all the way out here?*

That was the real reason that Lilleth wanted Hayden back in the city—she wanted to be able to keep a constant eye on her. Ever since they were little, Paul had been blaming Hayden for every single thing that went wrong in his life.

If Paul got suspended at school for cheating on an essay, it was Haydens' fault for not making the essay sound more like him. If Paul got caught stealing, it was her fault for not being a better look-out for him. Not once in his entire life had he been made to actually answer for all the shit that he did. It was never, well why didn't he do his own homework? Or why did he think he needed to steal anything in the first place?

Two years ago, Hayden had taken up the part-time job of being one of Pauls' undersecretaries while she was finishing up her undergrad studies. He'd asked her to liaise on his behalf with the ATO because some of his income tax was being delayed. She'd been made aware of an investigation they'd launched into his department because a significant portion of the pre-allocated funds had disappeared.

After going through the books with the forensic accountant, she had quickly realised that Paul had been setting her up. Apparently, he had employed her as a full-time executive assistant, which was worth about a hundred-thousand dollars a year more than what she had been receiving. Knowing the bastard like she did, Hayden had immediately taken a copy of the evidence to Paul and demanded an explanation.

Hayden had filmed the entire exchange, having given context at the beginning of the video while in the elevator going up to his office. Even as she'd stormed out of his office, he'd had no idea that he had been taped until the following morning. Hayden informed him that night that she was going to do her best to ensure he never got access to public funds again. After which she had taken the footage over to channel nine and then posted it to YouTube herself to guarantee everyone saw it.

The scandal that had resulted was a very well publicised, but brief investigation, at the end of which he'd been asked to step down from office and removed from working within the public service again.

Thanks again to the fuckwits' who designed the Australian Federal System that draws a very distinct line between working for the Public Service and working for Parliament. Dickheads. She muttered to herself as she continued to mete out her anger into the crumbling earth.

Twelve

Hayden finally called it quits on digging the hole when she could barely lift her arms. Deciding that one of the frozen microwave dinners was the wisest choice, she went to bed long before the sun had begun to sink.

Jason arrived the next morning, he was towing something truly extraordinary.

"I thought with Yule fast approaching, and your attention needing to be elsewhere—this might come in handy." He called out, as he slowly reversed his land-cruiser.

"Oh my Gods!" She squealed as she looked over the portable bathroom he'd brought with him, "you are the most incredible being on the face of the earth right now!"

"All you'll need to get her up and running is an outdoor extension lead—like this one," he added, holding up an orange cord, "and an outdoor tap."

He took another look over Hayden and quickly asked, "I can move it 'round to the water tank if you'd like so we can just set it up now?"

"You have no idea how incredible you are, do you?" Hayden asked rhetorically, as she beamed, "Yes, that would be amazing –you do that and I'll plug the cord in and lead it out the bathroom window."

In what felt like no time at all, Hayden was immersed in steaming hot water. Ensuring she was thoroughly clean, she hurried to get back to her guest. Who was already helping himself to the coffee and had brewed a fresh pot.

"Feel better?" he asked as she sat at the table beside him.

"Gods, yes. You have no idea how much." Hayden laughed as she took a sip, and sighed, relaxing even further.

"I'm starting to, everything okay out here? You looked wrecked."

Again, that show of concern speared her, her heart threatening to lose the fury she still held after the conversation with her mother the previous morning.

"Yeah, everything out here is fine—it's my mother in Sydney that's the issue. She called yesterday and it set me off. On the plus side I did manage to finally make a decision, I started digging the hole for the pool yesterday after the call." The admission came surprisingly easy.

"Well that's healthy." Jason commented.

"Hey, I was digging the hole for the pool—not because I was going to murder her."

"No seriously, I think you made the healthy choice there. Realistically, you could have done any number of things, yet you chose something both productive and constructive—despite the seemingly destructive nature of it all." His calm, steady demeanor was as open and honest as ever.

"Well then, thank you, I don't know what it is—but she just does not want to hear a word against her precious little boy. It's always been like that, and every single time she knows he's about to fuck it all up, she brings me in to keep an eye on him. It's like she wants me to take the fall for him every time he does something stupid."

Everything spilled out then, all the times that Hayden had taken the fall or been ostracised by her family because she refused to do it. All the pain just fell out of her. Jason didn't interrupt, he just sat there listening and letting her feel everything without judgement.

"What is it that she wants from you now then? You made a pretty damned public exit from his professional life—we rewatched the original clips the other day at work." he admitted.

"It's okay, and yeah I did. That's what she wants me to fix—she called me up yesterday morning, and said that Paul had graciously agreed to forgive me for my trespasses against him by allowing me to work for him again."

"Oh fuck that!" he instantly responded.

"My sentiments exactly, and Lilleth the great and powerful over there, did not take that very well." Hayden replied, widening her eyes for drama. "No, as a result of turning down the position that would force me to move back in with her, she says I now also have to host Yule lunch for my family, while also running the Yule Fair in town."

"You could just bring them in with you —I'll make sure Siobhan doesn't rip your brothers' head off. I can't make any promises about Patrick though, if he wants to do something—there's fuck all anyone can do to stop him." he joked back.

"Oof, as tempting as that offer is, it's not you guys I'm worried about—it's them. As awful as you think they are, they're ten times worse than that. I don't want them spoiling Yule for everyone." Hayden let out in a huff, "if by the grace of all the Gods, we actually do manage to get all the stalls set up, and everyone working together then there is no way I'm going to ruin it all by bringing my family."

"You do realise that you aren't supposed to feel that way about your family, you know?" Jason set down his cup and tilted his head as he waited for her to look back.

"Yeah I know, but how can I appreciate these people when I know that they actually will, want to ruin the fun for everyone—as long as it gets them what they want, which right now is to force me into moving back into the city, they'll do anything."

"That's not what I mean. Look at Patrick, Dan, Siobhan and I, we're nothing alike, but we are a family." he began, "as a great man once said, 'family don't end in blood'"

Hayden screwed up her face at the last comment, "did you just quote Bobby from Supernatural?"

"Yep, what? He was a great man—actually the actor still is, but the character," he put his fingers to his lips in a chefs' kiss before he continued, "absolutely brilliant!"

"I'm not denying that in the least, but I would have thought it would be incredibly insulting to you guys." Hayden asked, still a little taken aback.

"Nah, not as much as you'd think, for me at least. It's just like every other tv show out there, a fairly exaggerated one—but that's what makes it so inoffensive." He laughed back.

"So, you wanna show me this hole you dug yesterday?" Jason asked as he pushed his chair back to get up.

"Definitely, although I should prepare you, I was not in a good state while I was digging." Her teeth showed as she bit her tongue, and squished her face.

As they reached the spot where Hayden had started digging, Jason took a critical look at the area she'd wound up choosing.

"It's actually not that bad, to be honest." Jason commented as he inspected the hole she had started.

"Really? Well great, now I can cross successfully not fucking up digging a hole." The sarcasm rolled right off her tongue, shocking even her.

Jason turned, eyes wide as he laughed, "You've been hanging out with Siobhan too much."

"Maybe, but I think the opposite might just be true." She said as she spun her shovel in the air.

A short while later they had actually managed to dig a decently sized border ditch. Aside from taking a break for lunch about halfway through digging it out, they worked solidly right into the evening. It was the first time she experienced how fun doing mundane things with friends could be. Usually she would be anxious, instead, Hayden spent the entire afternoon singing karaoke into her shovel while Jason danced away to the music they blasted as they worked.

"I'm calling it, as it is I'm going to be fucked tomorrow—thank the Gods all I have to do tomorrow, is sit down in meetings all day." Hayden said as the battery finally died on Jasons' phone after using it as a speaker all afternoon.

"That's fair, I can't be fucked to work without music either, though I can appreciate the fact that I wasn't the one singing all day." He laughed as they walked back to the house.

"Thank you so much for today Jason, seriously, the way that everyone has been these last few weeks—it means everything to me. I just wanted to say thank you." She shrugged with her arms around her, as Jason climbed into his car.

"I know, we all do. We get it though, coming from a family like yours, I get it. We love you too." With that he pushed the button to wind up his window and smiled. Waving as he pulled away from the house and heading for the highway.

"Asshole!" Hayden laughed as she watched him go.

Thirteen

F riday morning dawned beautifully as Hayden watched it rise from her garden table—Hayden had actually managed to get a decent nights' sleep. It was still surprising that she slept so well out here, so far away from the rest of the world. The only time her internal clock seemed to be off was when Lilleth called.

One full day of literal emotional healing went a long way out here, and she loved it! The thought of her mothers' arrival, even a few days off, was still enough to spoil the sunrise.

Walking back inside, Hayden could have sworn she spotted a four-legged animal taking off around the corner of her house. Standing there, biting her lip, she was tempted to go after it, just to see if she could snap a photo. A quick glance at the time had her walking straight through the house—despite her early morning, Hayden was running late again. *Damned distractions, ugh, I wanna go chase the danger-puppy*, she internally whined as she started the SUV.

As beautiful as ever, the drive into town was a whole experience—having been introduced to most of the farmers' lining the highway into town with Siobhan. Entertaining herself, she practiced remembering the names of all the farms' managers and owners with their faces as she drove past their farm. Giving herself extra points if she could also remember their main crop or produce.

"You are never going to guess what arrived yesterday afternoon." Jason announced as she entered the bookstore.

"You're kidding." She smiled as she ran forward, excited.

"Here is mocha number one," he said as he handed her a mug, as well as a Yule-themed Borrow Me travel mug, "and mocha number two, this one's extra hot, so it'll still be warm when you and Daniel get to the council offices. They close at one for the entire week before Yule."

Dan, making his way over from the sales counter, was tossing a book up and down as he walked. "Literally the one day you plan to not come in, and it arrives." He laughed as he did so.

Hayden snatched it on his next toss, gliding her hand across the cover—still in its plastic sleeve. She loved this bit, being the first person to actually touch the pages. It was a thing only an archivist could really understand. Remembering that she was not in fact alone, her face shone red, and her eyes wide, Hayden slowly raised her head.

"You saw nothing!" She spluttered loudly, before taking off to stash *Plumbing for Dummies* in her car.

As purple as a beetroot, Hayden took a deep breath and walked back into the bookstore.

"You know, maybe we should get an extra copy for the store after all." Ricki suggested smoothly from behind the pastry fridge.

"With the way she just reacted to it, apparently the rainwater tank isn't the only thing with a busted intake pipe." Siobhan replied as she followed her in.

"Oh my Gods, it's not porn guys we've been through this—you didn't even like my porn collection, remember?" Hayden reminded them as she took a seat at her now favourite booth.

"Don't sit down, we have four meetings in the next two hours!" Dan worried.

"There is an actual reason I gave you a to–go cup." Jason observed.

"Then why did you also give me a mug?" she whined as she exited the booth.

"Well, you usually polish off the first one in three-point-five seconds—but then again I didn't factor in you treating a plumbing guide like it's the latest Marie LeFort book."

Feeling called out a little too hard for eight a-m, Hayden simply glared back as she skulled the mug of mocha, almost scolding her throat in the process.

Jason just smiled, and raised his eyebrows in expectation, holding out his hand for the mug.

"Rude," she smiled up at the bovine face before her and placed the mug in his hand, "accurate, but rude."

"No you were right, she really has been spending too much time with Siobhan." Daniel beamed at her.

Smiling proudly at Siobhan as they left the store, Hayden enjoyed the comforting familiarity. Daniel caught her up on the plans for the Fair in the car ride over to the council office. Essentially, Siobhan has been on the phone with each of the farmers they'd spoken to—and had eventually managed to get a hold of Terry. Everyone had said that they wouldn't be the reason, that the community would be let down.

"Well that's one giant weight lifted, fuck. I was freaking out the other day, I could have sworn they were all going to tell me to fuck off immediately if I'm being honest." Hayden admitted as they pulled into the carpark.

"Oh I get it, trust me—it's not always been sunshine and rainbows babe, but at least in this small corner of the universe, people are good more often than they suck. Which isn't as bad as I thought it was going to be."

"Does it get easier to handle? The whole sensory overload of people being nice—does the niceness back off? Or will I change to not be so weird about it?" She asked meekly.

He stared toward the buildings' entrance for a moment, took a deep breath and answered honestly, "it takes longer than you'd like, but one day, yeah—the meltdown and wanting to burst into tears the moment someone is nice to you, it won't be there. But you're human, and the gift of your people is that life is fleeting." He turned in the drivers' seat so he could face Hayden clearly before continuing, "so remember to soak in every second of peace and joy you can in this world, you don't have as long to enjoy it for."

As he turned to reach for the car door, she remembered her conversation earlier in the week with Siobhan.

"Dan, wait a sec—you and Siobhan are related right?"

"Kind of, her mum was a dryad who once had a thing with my dad for a bit, but we're not exactly from the same generational line if that makes any sense at all?"

"Not really," she admitted, "but that's not overly important, the point is, you care about her like she's your little sister right?"

Daniel raised his eyebrows eagerly, "oh really, well in that case—yes, Siobhan is exactly like my little sister."

"Ew, no, down boy!" Haydeb scolded as she caught his drift. "No, did you know that she wanted to be an Indigenous Rights lawyer?"

The dramatic shift in topic had Daniels' head tilted sideways and staring out the window once more as he searched through his memories.

"I remember she said something like that when she was still a sapling, but I take it she's said something more recently then?"

"Yeah, the other day—Dan I don't claim to know anything about your family or what she's been through. But I wanted to know what your opinion might be if I contacted an old friend of mine at Australia National University. It's only a couple of hours away, so she can literally just come home if things get weird or if they suck, and it's so much quieter than any of the uni's in Sydney."

Dan faced her once more, though Hayden could see the confusion, she had no way to decipher his expression to see if he was happy or pissed about her suggestion. Hoping for the former, Hayden bit her lip while waiting for him to reply.

Scrutinising her for any possible alternative purpose to sending Siobhan to the nations' capital, finding nothing but hope in Haydens' face, his own expression softened.

"How close are you and this friend? Could you get her private on campus accommodation? She'll want the security of having the campus police always on hand, until she gains a little more confidence anyway."

Relief flooded though her, and for the first time in front of another person, she let the tears overflow with ease.

"Well, she's one of the university's indigenous prodigy lawyers—so I'm pretty sure we can get that in place for her."

Despite the anxiety Daniel had clearly had earlier that morning about making it to their appointments with the councillors on time they however, expressed no such excitement.

The councillors had decided that they were no longer going to let us have a series of appointments to convince each of the committee members, no, instead Daniel and Hayden would now have to face an entire panel and convince them to approve all the permits simultaneously.

So what was supposed to be two hours of cajoling a few councillors, turned into a debate between them about what the overall cost to the town was going to be. Four hours later they had finally emerged from the council offices, not because they were done, but simply because it was time for lunch. If they didn't get the permits today, the entire event was going to be shut down.

"Does anyone want a coffee, on me?" Dan called over to them. Four of the six nodded, and agreed to meet over at the bookstore.

Calling ahead to give Jason the heads up, Hayden drove Dan's ridiculous sports car to Borrow Me's Café—*Who drives sports cars around country towns?* She'd noted internally, as they raced to get back.

"You were right—I should have just taken the coffees and pastry's like you said." He sighed into the speaker when the line connected.

"Told ya, Kaz did the stupid after she found out last night didn't she?" Jason snickered.

"Okay, okay, you can put the dicks away now boys remember that this isn't about you—it's for the town." Hayden reminded them.

"Right, who'd you get to come?" Jason intoned over the car's speaker.

"Henry, Taggart, Chelsea and Cameron. I don't think Kaz and Dick are going to swing by –but we'll have the vote without them." Daniel explained.

"Shit, are you going to do some witchy-woo-woo to their food?" Hayden freaked.

"What no?!" Jason and Daniel exclaimed together.

"No, we just know their orders off-by-heart. Between the food, and talking about how much fun it's going to be for the families who wouldn't have a holiday without it." Hayden relaxed her shoulders at Dan's words, as she pulled into a park close to the entrance.

Another hour later, and the receptionist in the town hall was printing off all the permits they would need.

"Want to double check we have them all before we go?" he asked as they looked over the pile of papers in front of them.

"Yeah, we should. Let's just bring up the list—we need the beef supply permit, and cooking in a public place for the Browns'" she began as she read the list off her phone.

Fourteen

The weekend that followed was one of chaos and stress to say the least—but nothing could beat Sunday, as she spent the day helping to decorate the towns' main street with the Borrow Me crew.

Jason and Ricki had been let in on Haydens' surprise Yule gift, and they had been excitedly putting together a study chest. Kind of like a glory box, but filled with academic supplies and near endless amounts stationary.

What Siobhan did though, brought everyone to tears.

"Hey guys, I'm going to head off quickly and get the last of the decorations from my place, to take them to the store—you got this?" she'd asked as they had been finishing up with the holiday bunting.

"Sure thing, there's not much left to do, and thank you again for helping out. I know you kind of pushed me into this—but seriously, I am never going to stop thanking you for all the help you've given me the last few weeks. You are incredible."

Siobhan had disappeared, only to truly surprise everyone when they walked into the store a short while later, and found a large potted Eucalyptus that had been meticulously decorated.

"Ta-da." She opened her arms wide, gesturing to the incredible sight before them. How she had managed to get it inside would forever be a mystery to her. Nevertheless, Hayden was astounded, and stood with her mouth gaping for so long that Ricki closed it for her.

"You best keep that one closed darl, not unless you're trying to catch some extra protein." He laughed as he walked over to Siobhan, and whispered something into her ear—causing her to blush and nod her head.

"I'm not going to ask, I have just one thing to say—you are incredibly beautiful and I can't wait to see how you continue to grow." Hayden said as she admired the Eucalypt. The tears shining in Siobhan's eyes, showing the depth of her understanding.

"Do you guys want to do a little Borrow Me gift exchange tonight? I'd rather do it on Yule—but with my family coming, I'm not sure I'm going to even be in the mood to celebrate." Hayden asked everyone when they'd sat down at the booth.

"I don't mind doing it tonight, all the gifts we buy, we hide here at the store anyway, and go hunting for them on Yule. Who's with me?" Dan shrugged.

"Ugh after all the prep cooking I've done today? Absolutely not, I'd rather tell you where your presents are and you can just go get them, but I'm not fucking hunting through the store for anything." Ricki dismissed.

"I don't mind helping you collect them, but I think I'm a bit overdone on the games for today." Jason puffed out—he had spent the entire day distracting everyone's kids. Enough families helping to get the town ready for the Yule Fair, had kids so he'd volunteered to make a temporary creche with a couple of the mums.

"Yeah, I'm sorry dude, but my mortality is killing me—especially my legs, so that's gonna be a hard pass." Hayden added.

Swinging his head from side to side, he shrugged his shoulders and went off in search of presumably his own gifts.

"You know, that's probably gonna get really annoying, really quickly." Hayden said slowly, as she stared after Daniels' receding form.

"Yeah, it does—so where's my present?" Siobhan begged, excitement lighting her features, while deepening the whorls etched in her skin.

"I figured I'd hide yours in the one place you wouldn't look—the boot of my car." Hayden stated, holding up her car keys.

The three of them smiled at one another, watching as Siobhan raced for her SUV, quickly following after her. Finding Daniel had already beaten them, nearing as he was handing Siobhan the chest of goodies Jason and Ricki had been putting together.

"What did you do? Run, run as fast as you can?" Ricki's sing-song comment went completely ignored, as everyone else watched as Siobhan opened the chest.

"I don't understand—what's with all the textbooks and shit." She asked, lifting her head to find the large envelope Hayden was holding out.

"This should explain it."

What seemed like an eternity of silence followed, while Siobhan read the offer of study from ANU.

Daniel had helped Hayden to steal her previous school transcripts—apparently she had been secretly, even unbeknownst to Dan, trying to study part-time online. According to her lawyer friend, Campbell, Siobhan's work was immaculate, it just seemed like she would lose her drive over, and over again. They all hoped that with a support team in place both at the uni as well as here, this time she'd have the drive to finish. All everyone wanted was to help Siobhan to have her best chance to do whatever it was that she wanted to do.

Daniel and Hayden took turns explaining everything that would be involved, if Siobhan decided to accept ANU's offer.

"I don't know what to say—I wish I could stay but, apparently I'm needed elsewhere temporarily. Uncle, are you okay with me doing this?" she squeaked uncertainly.

"Of course, I want you to be happy, Shiv. And as much as I love you, you are meant for so much more than this world realises. I can't wait to watch you show them how badly they've been fucking everything up." He replied emphatically, taking her into his arms. Everyone came in for that one, even Ricki had shed a few tears—one, still trailing tracks down his cheek as he buried it into the back of Dan's shoulder.

Yule eve was as mad as the day before had been, but without all the fun the previous night had had. In the end Hayden had stayed in town, crashing on Siobhan's' couch. At one point though, she was certain that was going to be a limited situation.

" Well now I know why you don't drink, and it's not because you're a bad drunk." Siobhan had informed her that morning—barely audible over the loud thumping that was pounding in her ears.

"Nope, it's 'cos I get super fucking annoying, and everyone usually avoids me after."

"What?! No—it's because you're an expensive drunk! It took both of bottles of tequila to get you shitfaced last night, and that is just plain rude not to tell someone." she had scolded.

"Wait, what?! That's what everyone's issue was all these years, the fact that it normally does nothing for me?" Hayden asked, her eyebrows scrunched in confusion.

"Yes! We are Australian, drinking is in our culture—you can't just go around to parties without bringing at least enough alcohol for you to get drunk, especially when it takes so much. I mean you don't have to drink that much obviously, but you really should warn people." The seriousness in her tone genuinely made Hayden think for a hot minute.

"Oh my Gods," Siobhan began, interrupting Haydens' reverie, "you must be really hung over this morning—I'm sorry, I thought you could interpret my tone, I was joking Sweets. I don't care about the booze, no one ever does, and the ones that do are dicks and they're probably addicted."

"Oh thank fuck, you had me going for a second there."

When the hangover haze finally cleared, she'd already driven halfway home—still needing to get the house clean for her family's imminent arrival.

Fifteen

The house was ready, well, as ready as it was going to be this year. All she could do was hope that there were enough Wattle trees around to send her mother straight back in her car.

Dressed in what she hoped would be considered an 'appropriate outfit' she checked the time on her phone again. They were late—and not a little late, a lot late. If they didn't arrive within the next ten minutes, Hayden was going to have to leave, and simply hope that they were safe.

Going back inside to collect her bag, she heard what sounded like a bunch of trucks honking their horns. Running outside to find her own driveway packed with tractor after tractor hauling large trailers—from the smell coming from them however, was absolutely repugnant. In the middle of the drive though, she could see her mothers' little Toyota Corolla appearing to be stuck between two of them. Doing her best not to burst into laughter at the realisation that Lilleth had been forced into the centre of a literal shit convoy.

Polly jumped down from the seat of the tractor in the front of the line, as the familiar sight of Jasons' hulking form ambling forward—-actually dwarfed by his surroundings for a change.

"I hope you don't mind," Siobhan yelled over the sound of tractor engines from next to him, "but I might have told a few people what you would want for Yule this year."

"Oh? And what exactly did you decide on?"

"About a hundred tonnes or so of steaming hot shit?" Polly yelled, a smile stretched across her face.

"Are you serious?!" Hayden yelled, everyone looking concerned and confused as she looked from one to the next. "That's fucking brilliant! Oh thank fuck, I have no idea what to say beyond thank you. Thank you, thank you, thank you!"

Hayden pointed the tractors to a particularly deser-tified paddock, and as the tractors moved the line along, her mother, along with her brother, and cruel step-father continued to make their way ever forward. The condemnation they gave as they got out of the car was palpable—scorn and disgust written all over their faces.

"Ugh, and whose stupid idea was it to get a delivery of shit for Yule?" Paul griped as he neared the crowded front door.

"Can we get away from this stench?" Lilleth demanded, pure disdain in every syllable.

"Yeah, why don't we go inside, the A/C's on and the lounge is so comfy you'll fall asleep." Hayden suggested to the group with an uncomfortable laugh. Turning to Ricki, she asked him to keep an eye on the tractors moving in and out.

"It's certainly interesting, I'll give you that." Lilleth remarked on the interior, her face set in a sneer.

The whole point of the yellow was to put her off, at the very least it had done that. Apparently, there seems to be a checklist of things you can do to make sure that your parents never want to visit—step one is to run away, step two is apparently have a hundred tonnes of shit literally escort them through the town, and lastly have completely terrible taste in design and really piss off your mother.

"So, where's Nan and Pop?" She asked, curious.

"Hayden, I know this is your house and it's by your rules that we must abide—however, you do know how I feel about animals on couches dear, the smell just never quite leaves." Lilleth said as she squinted her eyes in Jasons' direction.

"Oh fuck no." Hayden muttered, "You are not starting with that bullshit, not here, not now." she warned sternly. Adding in a softer tone, "Guys why don't you head back into town, and get changed for the Fair. We won't be far behind."

Siobhan pursed her lips and touched Haydens' shoulder in gentle support before walking back out the front door, where Ricki now stood—his eyes glowing and face darkening with a twisted smile.

"The last tractor is unloading their haul now, so the driveway should be free and clear in a few more minutes. Looking good Sis, that what you're wearing today?" Ricki informed them, before answering his own rhetorical question.

"It's gorgeous, I'll see you in a bit." He said as he poked his translucent head through the wall next to the door—eliciting a squeak out of her mothers' precious Paulie.

She had to purse her lips, and bite the inside of her cheek to keep from laughing at her familys' apparent fear of her friends.

A quick apology for her mothers' behaviour to Jason, and they were on their way again. Dan hadn't said a word the entire time, just stared at Paul as if he were dreaming of slaughter. *Actually, it was probably a good thing that they went back to town*, Hayden thought to herself making her way back to the house after seeing them off.

Her mother, step-father and idiot brother stood next to their car expectantly.

"I don't understand why you're acting like that, they're just people." Hayden stated, flabbergasted at the way her mother had spoken about her friends, as if they hadn't also been in the room, and capable of hearing.

"People, are fellow humans, darling. Those things," she pointed to the car turning onto the highway, "are *Creatures*, barely more civilized than that flock of chickens over there." Lilleth lectured.

Hayden had heard enough—whether any of them had said another word she didn't hear it, wouldn't, couldn't. Not over the deafening roar that now sounded in her ears, they could say what they wanted about her, she didn't care, but her friends? Absolutely-the-fuck-not!

"Well, whether you choose to acknowledge it or not Lilleth—they are people, my people!" She began, using her mothers' own name to her face as she finally confronted her bully. "You can leave, immediately."

"I'm fucking serious, I'm done, get out, get out of my house, out of my town, and out of my life!" Hayden screamed when they still didn't move to collect their belongings from inside.

Having said what she had always wanted to, she stormed inside, grabbed their bags—still piled up on her couch, and tossed them out her front door. While her toxic family ran to save their things, Hayden locked her doors. Then climbed into her SUV and left them to eat her shit-covered dust as she took off.

The last sight she had of her blood kin, was the most freeing moment of her life—she felt lighter than air, while they looked sore and covered in shit.

Her friends had been waiting for her, with a seat saved between Siobhan and Polly—a plate already loaded and waiting for her.

"Didn't save any seats for my folks did you?" she asked, scooting her chair closer to the table.

"No. You didn't actually bring them did you?" Dan asked, looking perplexed.

"Oh Gods no, they're either still trying to pack up the bag that flew open as I tossed it out the door, or already headed back to Sydney with shit all over them." She explained as she took a bite of Terry's famous smoked brisket. The taste washing away any ounce of regret that Hayden might have held on to, entirely.

"So, you gonna tell us what happened or what?" Ricki coaxed.

"Of course I will—just not today. Let me have the rest of today without having to think about them for another second."

"Sis, you don't have to think about them, ever again." Siobhan observed with brows raised.

And with that Hayden smiled, joyous tears filling her eyes as she looked around at the people surrounding her.

Stalls lined the street, a petting zoo at one end of the street with pony rides at the other for the kids. Someone had even brought a few mini tractors in for them to take turns riding. The people she had met over this last week alone, all laughing, smiling and nodding their thanks to her.

Hayden turned to the friends she now had, the family that she had found for herself, still surprised, amazed and entirely certain of just one thing...

"It's a lie you know, that voice in the back of your mind—the one telling you that you don't deserve it. That's her voice, and the lie that she told you."Polly's voice whispered in her ear, "you do deserve it, the friends, the family and us. Thank you, for being you, and for choosing to be here."

www.ingramcontent.com/pod-product-compliance
Lightning Source LLC
Chambersburg PA
CBHW040229170726
48295CB00014B/851